I0611784

HURT NO MORE

CHARNICE COLE HOGANS

HURT NO MORE

All rights reserved.

No part of this book may be reproduced, stored in a retrieval system, or transmitted by any means, electronic, mechanical, photocopying, recording, or otherwise, without the prior written permission from the author.

Unless otherwise indicated, Bible scriptures are taken from the KING JAMES VERSION (KJV): KING JAMES
VERSION, public domain.

Copyright 1994 by Zondervan

Copyright 2012 Merriam-Webster, Inc. Used with permission

Ordering Information:

ISBN: 978-1-7349358-2-0

Copyrighted Material

Printed in the United States of America

DEDICATION

I dedicate this book to two special women that had greatly impacted the process and creativity of this book. My mother and grandmother, you both are missed dearly. I love and miss you more than words can say; you'll always be in my heart.

ACKNOWLEDGEMENTS

First and foremost, I would like to thank my Lord and Savior for this opportunity to give birth to this project. Without HIS love, protection and guidance, this would not have been possible. I give Him all the Praise, Glory & Honor.

To my Beautiful Mother, the late "Lillian E. Cole," your life experiences, trials and tribulations prepared me for some of the brawls of life. Mom, you left this world so soon, but your elegance and legacy will forever be with me in my heart & soul. I will always LOVE you!

To my Warm Grandmother, the late "Thelma L. Cole," your wisdom has made me the woman I am today. I expressed this project to you many years ago. I recognize you for the inspiration to complete it. Thank you for all the encouragement and reassurance. You will always be my ROCK.

To my Beautiful children Robert III, Caleb, Joshua, and Arielle, I am EXTREMELY proud of the four of you. You all have always been my drive, motivation with unlimited tenacity & energy to keep it moving. You ALL are my heartbeat. I Love & Adore you very much.

To my Gentle Daddy, a supportive man that means so much to me & Mom, thanks for your love and support. I love you both very much.

To ALL my Lovely Sisters, I Adore & Appreciate you. Thank you so much for Your inspiration, comfort & ambition to keep moving forward & not to give up. That means the world to me.

To Everyone dealing with the struggle of FORGIVING, I inspire you NOT to let the pain or devastation in life stop or obstruct you from LIVING it to the fullest. There are countless people damaged mentally, emotionally, physically & spiritually because of past and current hurts. You can be HEALED! Allow God to restore your broken heart, the agony & every discomfort that has taken place. HE is the Answer and the Way!

TABLE OF CONTENTS

INTRODUCTION

Read this before you get started.

Have you ever been betrayed, violated, devastated and or rejected? The Hurts, Wounds and Pains are REAL! In life, everyone deals with some type of distressed feeling. It may be emotional, physical, mental, and or spiritual. Your story, time frame and title may be different from others. That painful feeling of agony and suffering is never pleasing.

This is a factual subject that is not dealt with head-on. Many of your devastations have been swept under the rug as if they would vanish and never be recognized. God has determined as he said in Luke 12:2-3, that the secrets will be uncovered and the truth will come forth, and God's thought about every behavior and action will be vindicated.

What's done in the dark will be brought to the light, and thanking God is imperative, knowing that this is His doing. Know that difficulty does not last forever. You can be healed, changed and set free. You may think the offense is too big to forgive. Forgiving is the way to not allow the past to hold you a prisoner to your own pain.

The best thing to do is let it go and not hold yourself hostage in the prison of unforgiveness. Holding on to the pain and blaming others hurts you more than it hurts them. Have a made-up mind to release it. Meditate on the Word of God and know that there is much Power in Prayer! Your life will never be the same after reading this book.

The author endured much hurt and pain but refused to allow it to keep her perplexed and at a loss. She was down for a moment but aroused with a made-up mind to fight back. She put on her boxing gloves and war clothes to go to battle against the adversary. You can do the same. The chains of hurt, bondage and unforgiveness can be broken off of your life. You will learn and know that with God/ The Supreme Being on your side, nothing is impossible to be handled. He is the way and the light.

CHAPTER ONE

THE PAIN FROM DISAPPOINTMENT

It was on a warm summer night in 1976, the stars were shining bright, a pleasant breeze blew through the bedroom window as the sheer white curtains whispered quietly. A six-year girl by the name of Shelly was soundly asleep when she suddenly heard a loud pounding noise from the front door. She heard the door open, then the voice of her mother screaming NO, NO! So, Shelly lifted in the bed with fear gripping her. She then jumped out of her bed to see what was going on with her mother.

To her surprise, she looked directly into the eyes of a man that looked familiar; he stood very tall over her 5'2 mom, wearing a black skull cap as he gripped and clenched her left arm tightly. Her mother yelled, "go back into your room now!" The little girl was extremely nervous and scared as she ran back into her bedroom; she began to cry as she grabbed her baby sister Toya out of the crib. Then she quickly hid in the back of her bedroom closet, holding the baby close.

Shelly quietly cried, listening to this man smack, beat, and punch on her mother. He thrust her mom into the bathroom, forcing her to take off all her clothes, telling her to put her head in the toilet. Shelly was without doubt afraid, continuing to hold her baby sister very tightly in her arms. Listening as her mother was forced back into the front of the house. Shelly paid close attention from her room closet as the house was being wrecked, the furniture being flipped over, her mom being mistreated and beaten, trying to stop this from happening.

The loud sounds of her mom screaming and crying, "I don't know what you are talking about," then this man hits her again. This abuse was awful for this little girl Shelly to witness. The bodily injuries by this obnoxious man that were intentionally taken place were devastating for Shelly. Trembling, quivering and crying, this little girl just did not know what to do. She is full of fear, wishing and hoping it would all just come to an end.

Once all the drama had ceased and she heard the front door close. Shelly stepped out of the closet apprehensively, not sure what to expect. She laid her baby sister back in the bed as she slept. Then she went to find her mother, looking at how the house was disarranged, broken glass and the disorder of all the furniture. Shelly found her mom laying on the floor nude with cuts and bruises all over her body, both of her eyes bruised, blackened and closed tight.

Shelly cried out, "Mommy, Mommy" shaking her repeatedly yelling, "Mom can you hear me?" Her mom was not responsive immediately, so Shelly began to uncontrollably shake her crying out "Mom" with the tears rolling down her face, "please mommy, please wake up." Without delay, she was awakened. Shelly pulled the blanket off the floor to cover her mom's body. Then she grabbed hold of her mother's hand and very firmly said, "I love you, mommy, please don't leave me."

Shelly looked into her mother's face, asking, who was that man? And why was he doing all those bad things to you?" Her mother tried lifting her body up, but the pain was so severe, she laid there whispering to Shelly, "I am ok, do you hear me? I am ok, I promise you." "Shelly, I don't want you to say anything to anyone about this," said her mother.

Extremely uneasy and perturbed, Shelly is weeping and frightened, not knowing what or why this has happened to her mother in their home. One should feel safe and most of all secure in your household. The feelings of disappointment and sadness have gripped the mind of this minor. The sight is disturbing for this child to try to digest as well as comprehend this. Shelly and her mother are in pain physically, emotionally and mentally, which has caused an unpleasant sensation for them both.

Here you see this child dealing with the sorrow, distress, and discomfort. Many people in the world today can relate to not knowing how to handle situations and or circumstances. This can cause much confusion and uncertainty. Your conditions may seem overwhelming, and you may feel that you are all alone. God is with you; He will carry you through every storm and give you strength

This six-year-old was feeling confused and scared, saying, "Mom, we must call for help; let me dial 911 so that the police can get that bad man." The appearance of her bruised and beaten mother laying on the floor in their home and the place being in disarray was truly difficult for Shelly to understand. She had never witnessed anything of this multitude in her short life. Shelly was a nervous wreck, knowing that if you call the police, they can help you. At least, that is what was taught to her by her mother and her teachers from school.

Indeed, she just did not understand how her mother can tell her everything was alright and for her not to tell anyone the things that had taken place in their home. Shelly realized she had seen that man a few times before, talking and laughing with her mother in the past. She really did not know him but wondered how someone could portray being nice to her mom but then be so mean and abusive. That was really hard for her to grasp and to try to understand. To keep quiet and not say nothing to anyone of what had taken place was distressing.

She just held on to it internally, just kept it inside, not knowing how it could affect her in the future. She was afraid of all this disappointment, often wondering if this would or could happen again. Disappointment is never fun, whether you're dealing with family, a relationship, work, or school. If you've missed out on a major prospect, a situation that didn't work out, it could be to advance your career or if it is chaos with your family or friends. No matter the disappointment, it's almost never as bad as it seems, and there are always more ways out than you may think.

It is imperative to let your feelings out, it is normal that you feel upset, troubled or even inconsolable. However, the distress and devastation are real; acknowledge it and accept your pain. Don't be ashamed to cry, scream, shout or otherwise express your feelings. This doesn't necessarily mean doing so in public. Though, letting out your emotions are healthier than suppressing them.

However, avoid lashing out at others, which could cause so much more stress. Praying and meditating on the Word of God is vital. It is key and critical to put the problem and issue in perspective. However, the experience of disappointment is profound, and the emotion of sadness is real, which can be felt and handled in many situations.

The feelings of distress and unhappiness comes from disappointment which is a painful or sad feeling that happens when something disrupts your positive feelings and hopeful expectations

In life, one will encounter circumstances and situations that may try to keep you stagnated, to the point you find yourself trapped and really do not know how to move forward. You cannot allow conditions or environments to permit you to feel stuck or imprisoned to the point you feel that there is no way of escape. One must stay focused so that you may advance & develop into the person and purpose God has for you.

Every child will experience pain at one time or another, whether from everyday bumps and bruises or more chronic conditions. Pain is one of the most misunderstood, neglected and unaddressed issues with children. This is real and pain can come in many manners and behaviors.

No matter where or how the pain or discomfort is brought about, it is important to talk about it, describe it, express what is going on despite your age. Find someone you can sincerely talk to about what's going on in your life, try to understand the actual issue, and not allow bravery to rule. Know that getting help to heal and ease the pain is crucial regardless of your age and gender. Shelly loves and adores her mother. She is feeling sad and down because of what has transpired.

Sadness is a painful emotion of disconnection from someone or something that you value or desire to value. It is important to know that sadness helps you remember rather than forget. The emotion of sadness attempts to assist you by giving you the opportunity to consider the effect of your pain and the necessity of revising your purposes and strategies for the future. Shelly is enduring much discomfort and not understanding the ways of life. She is at a young age, not knowing these circumstances are yet helping her for forthcoming life experiences.

Whether intentional or not, the effect on a child who is rejected, not fully understanding or not feeling fully accepted and important by one parent or both can be devastating. The result is often low self-esteem, chronic self-doubt, and or depression. Often the impact lasts well into adulthood.

> *"Disappointment to a noble soul is what cold water is to burning metal; it strengthens, tempers, intensifies, but never destroys it."*
>
> **– Eliza Tabor.**

Throughout your life, you'll be faced with many disappointments. Perhaps you're dealing with a disappointment right now. Whether someone you trusted and loved let you down, whether something in your work or business didn't go right, whether your life isn't where you want it to be, life just seems to have a way of kicking us when we're already down. Try to stay focused and know that with God on your side, He is the source and He has all power.

> **Disappointment is not an easy thing to face but standing strong in the face of disappointment and picking yourself up afterwards is crucial to living a good life.**

Shelly began to learn the things of life in terms of what is right and what is wrong, but then to see the contradiction of it was troubling. This caused disappointment, heartache, and confusion for her. She was a young nervous wreck, full of fear. As time went by, Shelly never repeated anything. She was just withholding so many emotions, as well as being unable to express her true feelings.

All she knew is that she loved her mother very much and did not want to see anyone or anything hurt her. Shelly did not want her mother to endure any type of pain, worry, or torment. Shelly just held all these concerns and anxieties within, kept it to herself just as her mother said. If that would help protect, guard and save her mother from any hurt, harm or danger, that is what Shelly had to do. Shelly was an obedient and respectful girl who tried to keep a positive attitude and a smile on her face.

Although, she was somewhat confused and not clearly understanding the overall situations in life thus far. Yet, by Shelly being so young, she was very mature for her age. She expected nothing but the best for their household. Shelly anticipated and expected that there should be comfort, well-being, and peace of mind in their home. Not knowing that there are debauched and wicked people in life, bad environments, hard circumstances, and tough situations.

Nevertheless, life difficulties and actions that occur may perhaps sometimes be evil, wrong and unsatisfactory, but one cannot allow it to regulate and dictate what your future holds. Shelly, at such a young age, was determined to see the good in all the ugly. She was submissive to those who had authority over her. In the midst of life situations, she tries to stay optimistic, being so young and not understanding or developing all that life brings. She took one day at a time dealing with the brokenness, hurt and the misunderstandings.

This little girl was weathering storms of life with the Lord on her side, not even knowing it. The Bible informs us about the protection of God. As humans, we want to see God's protection as a magic force field that keeps us from all harm. Yes, God can prevent any evil or destruction, but we must remember that we live in a fallen world where we have free will. Many times, God works in ways that we do not understand.

Sometimes God's protection comes in the form of peace and strength in the middle of despair and misery. It was revealed that Shelly's mother had been exposed to illegal drugs by a few family members and friends. Testing the waters could be very dangerous. The usage of the substance of drugs can affect the way the body functions. Knowing that illegal drugs have different effects on people and these effects are influenced by many factors.

This really makes them unpredictable and somewhat dangerous. As a child, Shelly was always told by her mother, "What goes on in my house, stays in my house." Shelly recalls expressing to her friends and the neighbors across the street some personal information from their home regarding her mother and a white powdery substance which was cocaine. The adult neighbor reported back to Shelly's mom everything Shelly discussed regarding her using hard drugs. Why did Shelly speak of and talk with friends about the white powder in their house that got her in some very bad trouble?

Drugs can be a factor in the home. Shelly's mom had connected with one of top drug dealers in the city. He was the one who introduced her to the usage of cocaine, pills and marijuana. Drugs are real and addictive. Some feel that they control their usage and stop when they feel like it or when they are ready. She was asked by her mother what was told to the neighbors about what was going on in her house.

Shelly suddenly knew she was not to repeat anything that was going on in their home. So, she was put on punishment and got an extremely bad whipping from her mom. However, she was definitely dealing with much confusion and misunderstanding when it came to what's right and what's wrong.

> *The surroundings you face may cause you to feel discouraged with a sense of impairment when it comes to your confidence as well as finding oneself feeling disappointment, distress and discover that in many fragments of your life, you seem to find yourself with regret or just not understanding.*

Shelly always lived with her mother and not her father. The two of them were young teenagers when Shelly was conceived, and the relationship did not work out as they thought it would. Still, Shelly was able to spend much of the time with her dad on the weekends. The overnight stays were very important to her because she felt she was treated her age and did not have so many responsibilities. Being a child and being able to relax as well as feel secure was something splendid to Shelly.

It was a tremendous difference for her in both of her parents' households. In her father's home, he was now married and had three more children. Shelly's two brothers and sister were younger. She was always so excited to go over there on the weekends to play with her siblings, friends next door, across the street and to also visit her grandmother. Her grandmother lived upstairs from her father in a two-family flat.

Shelly adored her grandma; she was a woman with lots of wisdom and knowledge. She was one that cherished her family and had marvelous stories to tell of her childhood growing up in the south. So, Shelly had plenty to do when going to her father's for the weekend. However, Shelly sometimes felt out of place while visiting, perhaps a little rejected or possibly shunned when it came to her siblings. Shelly periodically felt that she did not truly fit in at times.

Especially since she was her dad's oldest child by someone else, she perceived that she was sometimes treated differently from the way her sister and brothers were. In some cases, Shelly felt as if she was in the way of the perfect family as the outcast. She knew that her stepmother was not her biological mom; however, she sometimes felt that there was a difference in the way she was treated or dealt with compared to her siblings. Shelly being mature at such a young age, had the spirit of discernment; she just had the perception and insight of knowing if one was being genuine and real to her in different areas in her life.

She was very quiet but used her judgment and intuition in many situations as a young girl. There were times when she honestly felt so out of place; things were said to her at a young age that made her feel as if she was not 100% a part of the family, such as your daddy loves me better than he loved your mother by her stepmom. A few times, there were items Shelly would ask for on her birthday or Christmas; in return, it would always seem to be an imitation of it or one of her siblings will get the real thing. Shelly understood the difference in the mother's situation as a child; she knew she was truly loved by her father no matter what. Shelly never dwelled on it or spoke of it.

She internalized it and added on with the additional life situations she endured. Even so, as time went by, the good outweighed all the negative feelings. Shelly felt some of the wounds were healed. She refused to allow the feelings of sadness to dictate her hopes and expectations in life. Shelly was older and happy to be in a new environment, an innovative atmosphere, a place where in her mind, she had a feeling of pleasure, affection, and lots of love when visiting over her grandma's and daddy's house.

However, Shelly felt a sense of stability, safeness and protection from her dad no matter what was going on. He always showed her love, warmth, built her confidence up, and supported her in any activity that took place in her life. Shelly's dad was extremely supportive in all her endeavors. Nevertheless, when it came to Shelly and her parents, there was a way Shelly would respond to both houses when it was time to go. Just simply saying, I am ready to go home to be with my mom and sister, she would express to her dad. And to her mom, she would say, I want to spend time with my dad and the other side of my family.

That was her way of escape to each household. In life, everyone has dealt with or is dealing with sadness. It is a painful emotion of disconnection from someone or something that you value or you want to value. This feeling can cause grief, sorrow, and much heartache. This may have a huge impact on one's perception of the world.

> *We have all gone through something as a child with our parents or those that have authority over us. No matter what situations you may endure in life, your answer is in God, who is Love.*

Know that it is okay to feel disappointed, which may come with dealing with embarrassment, guilt and helplessness. These emotions and experiences truly caused Shelly to feel terrified and have disappointment. This shows that emotions are being taken on as disposition, character and one's temperament. Emotions can be quite overwhelming, making it difficult to concentrate as well as focus. Emotions are associated with physiological changes in the body. Shelly was dealing with changes in her body, far as being extremely nervous, fearful and very sensitive. She would break out with rashes on her neck, arms, and legs when these different issues would occur, that were not so great.

To help dismiss and aid Shelly with dealing with all these emotions was first of all, having peace of mind and most of all, prayer. If something or someone gives you peace of mind, it stops you from worrying about a particular problem or difficulty. Peace of mind is a state of mental and emotional calmness, with no worries, fears or stress. In this state, the mind is quiet, and you experience a sense of happiness and freedom. Such peaceful moments are not so rare.

Shelly did not know much about prayer, but she had some praying grandmothers who did not say much to her concerning her matters, but they knew something was going on with her and in the household. They prayed and encouraged her every moment they could. Prayer is a solemn request for help or expression of thanks addressed to God or an object of worship. It is an earnest hope or wish. It's an invocation or act that seeks to activate a rapport with an object of worship through deliberate communication.

Know that you can recover from disappointment. One may deal with hindrances, setbacks and burdens in the midst of your storm. It is important to face the truth of the situation. It is simply alright to allow yourself to mourn your lost family member, lost relationship and lost dream; no matter what your condition is, it is okay to feel the heartache and sorrow. There are moments when one may find themselves stuck or trapped in the victim mentally.

You feel powerless, unable to solve a problem or cope effectively. You may tend to see your problems as extreme misfortune and utter failure. You tend to think others are purposefully trying to hurt you. You believe you alone are targeted for mistreatment and one may hold tightly to thoughts and feelings related to being a victim. This is how the enemy wants you to stay and be conformed to this mindset. That's when one must check to see if your expectations are realistic, accurate and most of all truthful.

Being kind, caring, and generous to yourself is vital. Loving yourself tremendously, one should know that to love yourself means to accept yourself as you are and to come to terms with those aspects of yourself that you cannot change. It means to have self-respect, a positive self-image, and unconditional self-acceptance. Try to find and look for balance. Look for the good and try to emphasize the hopeful side of a situation that might seem gloomy on the surface.

It is important to know that whenever you are going through a hard time, try to remind yourself that "every cloud has a silver lining" means that even the worst events or situations have some positive aspect. Know that change, with transformation and trying different approaches, can enlighten and empower you greatly. Accept what has happened and know that what is done in the past cannot change. There are circumstances in life you may not understand, but God knows all things.

"But I will restore you to health and heal your wounds,"
declares the Lord.

Jeremiah 30:17

He gives strength to the weary and increases the power of the
weak. Even youths grow tired and weary, and young men
stumble and fall; but Those who hope in the Lord will renew
their strength.

Isaiah 40:29,31

Come unto me, all ye that labor and are heavy laden, and I
will give you rest.

* Matt 11:28*

The Lord will ease, relieve and refresh your souls. Casting all
your care upon him; for he careth for you.

I Peter 5:7

Give all your anxieties, worries, and concerns to God for He
cares for you lovingly and watchfully. Honor your father and
your mother, that your days may be long in the land that the
Lord your God is giving you.

Exodus 20:12

He healeth the broken in heart, and bindeth up the wounds.

Psalm 147:3

The Lord can cure all your pains, sorrows and
disappointments. A merry heart doeth good like a medicine:
but a broken spirit drieth the bones. Being cheerful keeps you
healthy. It is slow death to be gloomy all the time.

Proverb 17:22

*For I know the thoughts that I think toward you, saith the
LORD, thoughts of peace, and not of evil, to give you an
expected end.*

Jeremiah 29:11

*Be careful for nothing; but in everything by prayer and
supplication with thanksgiving let your requests be made
known unto God.*

Philippians 4:6-7

*Be strong and of a good courage, fear not, nor be afraid of
them: for the LORD thy God, he that doth go with thee; he
will not fail thee, nor forsake thee.*

Deuteronomy 31:6

PRAYER FROM DISAPPOINTMENT

Heavenly Father,

I am feeling down, and I come before you with a sincere heart. My life has not been what I expected; I have been sad and disappointed. Lord, I need your help; please help me let go of all the disappointments of the past and to forgive those that have hurt and damaged me so deeply. Keep me Lord and make me whole because I don't want to hold on to bitterness and have resentment in my heart. I want to be free from this because it is destructive to my peace and relationship with you. I give you praise and honor. Amen

CHAPTER TWO

THE WOUNDED MIND

A few years went by, some of the family members would say that Shelly was a lady in a little girl's body. She was very advanced for her age and smart in school. She was not the average little girl; she was left alone with her little sister and this was a lot in their home while her mother went out. Shelly would get busy trying to clean, wash, do the dishes, try to even cook, and even try sewing with a needle and thread. This little girl was adventurous; if she saw something needed to be done, she would try to do or fix it.

Shelly was very courageous and just wanted her mom to be proud of her with things around the house. Going from one house to the other was an advancement in things learned; it was a steady progress in acquiring and gaining skills from both sides of the family. Shelly learned much from the good, the bad and the ugly when she was in the presence of both sides of her family. In life, you will be faced with letdowns, dashing hopes and dissatisfaction; however, you cannot allow the feelings of displeasure, hurt, discontentment and/or pain to stop you from fulfilling your hopes and expectations.

You are here for a reason, with great purpose and perseverance in your life. Hurts, wounds and heartache can set in, but you must not allow it to rule or take over your mind. It is important to know that sadness and annoyance caused by the nonfulfillment of one's hopes or expectations can cause great disappointment. Shelly has many different emotions going on in her mind. She has dealt with and is dealing with these different feelings, which have been stimulating her parasympathetic nervous system.

This is a chemical response that can trigger melancholy and a feeling of hopelessness. She has encountered many emotions and reactions at such a young age; some of these extreme circumstances have had an abundant response to Shelly. There are ways to overcome disappointment, hurt, and a chaotic mind. To overcome sadness, it is imperative to recognize and acknowledge how you feel about the situation.

You must take time to question your anticipation of the overall affair. It is essential to take time to learn from the experience. Take a personal account of the situation. Adapt and try to adjust to the expectations and objectives. There are so many people broken inside in life, but despite their circumstances, they still manage to smile and sometimes portray that all is well.

For all those with secret pains, God will wipe away your tears. Know that it is okay to feel disappointed, which may come with dealing with embarrassment, guilt and helplessness. These emotions and experiences truly caused Shelly to recognize that she was a damaged girl who was terrified, trying to figure out and handle the wounds and hurts she faced thus far. Emotions can be quite overwhelming making it difficult to feel that one can freely express how they are genuinely feeling.

Shelly's mother met a man named Leon Otis, who seemed to really love and adore her. He really treated Shelly and her sister well. He always took them out to dinner, the movies, and would bring nice gifts once or twice a week. Shelly knew her mom was really headed over the hills for him. They trusted and felt secure in his presence.

Leon always kept a smile on their faces and treated Shelly's mother very well. Her mother began to care, rely on, and felt assured about this man; he treated them all with much kindness. As time went by, her mother began to allow Leon to stay with her girls until she made it home from work or whatever it was that she had to do. He always wanted Shelly to sit on his lap or between his legs, only when her mother was not around.

Shelly did not like that. He would always try to entice her with candy, money (coins) or even small toys. As a girl, Shelly would be excited about these things. However, she did not want to be too close to him. He would always rub and caress up and down both her legs and her little thighs.

He would also tell her to relax and rub her back, then across her private areas, the vagina and buttocks with her clothes on. She really felt uncomfortable with him touching her. Shelly would tell him "No, stop I am going to tell my mom." He informed her not to say anything to her mother or to anyone, and if she did, he would hurt her mother and her baby sister. This certainly made Shelly really upset and more confused.

As time went by, the rubbing turned into feeling inside of her panties then on her private areas. Kissing on her ears and down her neck, then eventually all over her body. He relished holding her tightly as if she was his property. This grown man after a period of time, got comfortable and content with violating this young girl. Pumping and humping on her very fast and hard.

He would constantly repeat to Shelly; this is our little secret; you better not tell anyone. She was extremely afraid and fearful, knowing that it was not right. Her mother always expressed to her that no one is to ever touch you in your private areas. She always repeated, "No one, it does not matter who it is and if it ever happens, you make sure you tell me." This is what was always told to her by her mother.

After all, Shelly wanted to make sure she protected her mom from being hurt. Shelly did not want to see another man putting his hands on her mother with any type of abuse or harm in any matter. Finally, something happened to him and her mom's relationship. They broke up and he wasn't around or seen anymore. This relationship connection was over between the two and Shelly was so delighted and excited, she never told anyone what had taken place from Leon Otis with the sexual abuse.

She tried to erase and remove it, but what she did was suppressed it. Shelly was glad that the association was no more. So, she felt that since he was gone, everything would be ok. Shelly was just glad he was not around any longer.

Dealing with life's heartache and pain is extremely important; many are sweeping situations and devastation of life under the rug. As if it never existed, trying to put it away, ignore it, not deal with it, hoping and praying that everything will get better and change. You may try to be oblivious to it, try to disregard it, or just turn a blinded eye or a deaf ear to it, whatever that situation may be. It must be dealt with.

At this point in her life, Shelly has been holding on to all this havoc and disorder that has been taking place in her life up to now. This young girl wants to be obedient and pleasing to her mother regarding the horrible offenses and destruction that had taken place prior in their home. As well as all the other wrongdoings she faced. She was holding on to this without anything being said or done. Shelly has suffered much in her lifetime so far. She wants to make sure her mother is protected from any more type of harm or injury to the best of her ability.

Not even realizing that she was the victim of it as well. It may seem as though circumstances in the household should not affect anyone but whom the damage happens to, which is not true. Everyone is involved; it is devastating to see a loved one or should it be said anyone suffer emotional, physical, and mental afflictions. You are not alone, so sweeping situations under the rug or trying not to talk about them is not the answer. As if it does not exist, wishing and hoping it will disappear. That is not reality.

To suffice or act in such a fashion actually hurts you rather than helps you. Shelly went through a lot growing up; she saw and heard much that one should not have. She grew up being very mature and family and friends always stated how responsible she was at such a young age. Shelly endured this pain of being molested by her mother's boyfriend and was told by him not to tell. She remembered her mom's abuse and beatings more than once and was told not to say nothing.

She remembers the usage and selling of drugs in their house. Their home was firebombed, and these were a few of the situations that she coped with. It is sad to experience all of this as a young child growing up. Again, these are issues that were swept under the rug, not being dealt with.

> *This could truly have a tremendous effect on one's existence, especially as you grow and mature in life*

In the real world of life, everyone will somehow experience some type of hurt and agony. You may not know exactly when it may occur, but it will. However, you cannot allow it or the situation to regulate or engulf you. Everyone is different and that is how God created us. We are all unique and special with our own personalized stories. There are many situations in your life span that will cause unhappiness and your mind to be wounded.

You may feel hurt, crushed, which may cause mental pain, being offended, and this can cause you great suffering. You must fight the good fight of faith, and you cannot quit. The Lord is able to do all things but fail. You must hold your head up in confidence, knowing that trouble doesn't always last forever, knowing the situation you are in is not permanent. We are all emotional beings and that is how the Lord made us. So, it is ok to be angry, discouraged, upset, etc.

However, you cannot allow your emotions to regulate or dictate how you feel, what you do and most of all, the way you react.

The discomfort and dissatisfaction are there, but you must not allow it to govern or dominate your life. You can do all things through Christ that strengthen you. The Lord is not a forceful God; he allows us to make choices. He wants to always guide us in the right direction, to prevail over all the traps the enemy sets. No matter what heartache, destruction, suffering you have endured, know that you can be totally healed, delivered and set free. One may realize or feel that they are in this battle and it is real; just know that your battles belong to the Lord.

The unpleasant situations caused much discomfort for Shelly. It had her really distraught. She was upset and sometimes agitated. These types of issues can cause one to lose their mind and even go crazy. Shelly did a lot of crying when she was alone.

She often found herself wanting to be alone, but it never really happened. Not knowing it at the time, Shelly was dealing with a form of stress. At such a young age, she was a nervous wreck. She was so fearful, did not know what was going to take place next. Just about every night before bed, she would lay there with her eyes closed tightly and make a wish that everything would be alright for all of them. Although she really had no idea of their actual conditions, Shelly just knew she did not want anything negative in their atmosphere.

If it was, she hoped and yearned for it to disappear and never come back. Shelly was so young, going through a lot; she had seen and heard so much. All she desired was that everything around her could be pleasant and primarily having a peaceful mind.

> *The mind is powerful in which it processes reasons, thinks, feels, wills, perceives and judges. Children begin by loving their parents at a very young age; as they grow older, they judge them, and sometimes they forgive them. It is important to try not to hold on to hurts. Releasing it instead of incorporating it is very important for the mind, body, and soul.*

Shelly is older now, in her early teens trying to leave the things of the past behind without ever actually dealing with them. She really did not know what to do or how to actually handle it. Constantly, thinking and hoping that everything she had endured could just disappear and be gone totally out of her mind. All that had taken place in her life thus far, she wanted it erased—the moving from house to house without much stability. The responsibilities of taking care of her siblings, along with cooking and cleaning, she was just a little lady in a girl's body with many responsibilities.

Her mother has had two more little girls, a set of twins, Veronica and Victoria. While her mom did her own thing, she was hardly ever home. She was constantly on the go and Shelly had the obligation of keeping the house in order to the best of her knowledge, along with taking care of her siblings. On top of all of that, Shelly was trying her best to do good in school. That was a very heavy load to carry, but she persevered through it all.

Shelly was a bright young girl who was determined to handle what needed to be taken care of. She worked hard in everything presented to her, despite what they did not have. There were times when the telephone was cut off, along with the lights and gas. This was something that occurred temporarily; however, they survive through it all. Again, she did have a place to escape to when everything seemed unbearable and overwhelming.

Shelly would call her father to come get her for the weekend. She would be excited about going away for those few days; this was a place where she would be treated her age, not like the little mom, with all those responsibilities. It was also time for her to play with her other siblings and her friends that stayed on the block and in the neighborhood. Shelly is now attending high school; she was accepted into this honorable and prestigious school where many had applied but few were chosen.

So, it was totally time to do nothing but focus and keep up a high-grade point average to make sure she would stay in this great school. She was attending school with a few friends from her elementary and middle school from the neighborhood. Shelly caught two buses to school early every morning, making sure she was on time for every one of her classes. Shelly was also excited to know that her father was an alumnus of this great school. He had attended and graduated from this school and she was so proud to tell everyone that they both had the same high school counselor.

The legacy and school bequest were moving on, and this was some positive and uplifting information for Shelly to be proud of and share. Everything seems to be going ok for her, and there were not too many things for her to complain about. Shelly had adjusted and was used to the drug usage from her mom, the crowd coming in and out of their house. After a while, her grades began to drop and she just could not focus. She really did not want to be removed or let go of her school because of her grades.

She found herself being frustrated and irritated, trying to work through the distractions in which she had done plenty of times before. This was getting harder for her each day and she understood that this was out of her control. Shelly realized her life was enormously different from her peers. Just talking and spending time with her classmates she grasped immediately that their lives, lifestyles were totally different. Although it is clear that everyone has their own story and issues.

In her eyes, it seemed that everything seemed great and all together for them as they would converse. They all seemed to have more stability and seemed to be more sheltered and the solidity in her eyes seemed so right. They all seemed to have had it all together and that is what Shelly always hoped for. This home situation was just too hard for her to bear; she complained to her mom, who was high on drugs most of the time and not totally committed to her children. However, she was devoted to that crack pipe, heroin and cocaine.

Shelly watched as her mother changed drastically before her eyes. The appearance, the responsibilities, the household, her girl's well-being and most of the things she would do for the drugs. However, one-night Shelly went down into their unfinished damp basement to try to concentrate on the project that was due for school. She cried out loudly, saying, "Why? & How? Can I do this?" To her surprise, she heard her uncle James come in the door upstairs. He asked her sisters, where is Shelly?

They let him know she was in the basement; he came down the stairs to see that she had been crying. He asked her what was wrong? She began to explain to him that she could not concentrate for school and that she could be at risk of being let go from the school if she did keep up with her grades. He hugged her tightly and told her it was going to be alright. Uncle James then said to her, "Shelly, go get all your belongings together so that you can go live with your grandmother." Who were his and her mom's mother?

He said to her; you can have my room; I'm hardly ever there. He then encouraged her, letting her know that she will not be kicked out of the school. He stated to her, "just get your things you're going to get back on track while staying with grandma." She is now there in her grandmother's home and was extremely grateful for her uncle James who seemed to always come to the rescue. He realized with his sister's lifestyle that his niece Shelly was unable to change it and had no control of the surroundings.

That environment was Shelly's reality; however, the modifications, a made-up mind, determination, and perseverance were vital for her. Shelly was back on track. Shelly is at an age where she wants to feel secure, safe and protected as well as believing everything will be better and well. She has stability and doing well in school, and she was so happy. Her focus has helped her grow, flourish and cultivate a new attitude to stay on the path of success despite the issues of life.

You may feel overwhelmed, rejected, abandoned, and may want to give up. You may go through different situations in life that you have no control over. You might feel like giving up and feel that you cannot tolerate it anymore. Bitterness will try to rise...know that being bitter is harsh, painful, resentful, mean, angry, cruel and spiteful. This is exactly what the enemy wants. Try to stay focused and centered.

You have been injured; your heart has been torn, pierced, cut or even broken. You try to surpass or try to forget what has happened to you. You are trying to go on with life as if nothing wrong has taken place. All these thoughts are in the mind and you are trying to erase them. You have to admit and acknowledge the issue first, then release it. Stop trying to hold on to it, exhale and let go of all that damage. Life will be so much better.

Shelly had to adjust and learn that there is another way of life. She connected with friends that encouraged and motivated her even though she never told them her story. It was now her junior year in high school, and she had grown. She was making her own little money from working a part-time job. She was feeling good getting her hair done, buying the things she desired.

It was this fine mid-height dark guy named Terrance, who was in Shelly's sophomore math that seemed to always pick with her and flirt with her. She knew he had a crush on her, and she realized she was crushing on him as well. They became a couple in their junior year of high school. The connection was great, they had so much in common and he always made her smile. They spent a lot of time together, had so much fun and no matter what, he always looked out for her.

He loved to shop for her, and he was always surprising her with nice things, especially on special occasions such as birthdays, Sweetest Day, Valentine's Day and those just because days. He had a special bond with her family, especially with her grandmother and her little sisters. He would always inspire, encourage and motivate her to keep going strong. He knew and understood her story; he knew some of the things she endured. He boosted her not to quit, give up, and always keep the smile on her beautiful face.

They definitely had a connection despite the relationship not lasting or working out. Terrance always stayed in touch with Shelly's grandmother and Shelly always kept in touch with his grandmother. Though the courtship was over, they were true friends, and there was no more contact between them anymore for a moment. They both did decide no matter what life brings them; they will always be friends. Now that Shelly was not living with her mom, she found herself focusing on her and watching her struggle with this drug addiction.

This crack cocaine had an effect that was unbelievable on her, along with dealing with other ailments in her body. Shelly has always tried to be strong, which is how her family always betrayed her to be. Being strong means choosing yourself even when people don't choose you. It means choosing to be true to yourself even when it hurts. Being strong was imperative and a necessity for Shelly.

She realized that strength helps build stability. However, Shelly felt wounded, suffering and anguish at times. She believed that staying strong meant she would have clarity in what she wanted out of life despite how and what she went through growing up. Staying strong means having a never-give-up attitude, no matter what. Staying strong means fighting it out, all odds.

Staying strong means challenging the routine. This was a part of Shelly's character and something that was instilled in her; she was just born with it. At this time and point in her life, it is important to try to confide or find someone she could trust to release or disclose all the drama that she had sustained. One may wonder who you can really trust that will pray with you, not judge you, encourage you to hold on and go through.

In the midst of all the different storms, the coping was terribly difficult at times. It is great to have a prayer partner and even better to have a prayer life of your own. Knowing God for yourself is extremely important. The enemy tries to have you succumb to this heartache; he expects you to wither away. The adversary is a liar and a deceiver with no victory.

Shelly has battled numerous wounds but tried to patch, bandage, stitch them up and keep it moving on her own. That is definitely not a good thing to do. A wound is a serious injury, especially a deep cut through the skin and it could be emotionally in the heart. Wounds are serious: we're talking a lot worse than just a scrape or booboo. Just about all the meanings of this word have to do with being hurt. Shelly has tolerated and bore the hurt for years now.

She's been ready for permanent change; however, there are changes that take place steadily in life. Most of us know that negative emotions aren't something one wants to experience. Know that it is about you being made complete and free from the scars from old. Accept yourself and your mistakes and most of all, learn from them, try not to continue to go down that same road. Doing something different and looking at the situation from another view really helps.

Accept what has happened and know that it cannot be changed; however, you can be transformed. It is imperative not to be isolated, inaccessible to others and the world. That is just what the enemy wants, so go out and be with nature. If you have any questions and or any concerns, do not be ashamed or reluctant to ask for help. Remember and know that no one can read your mind.

Shelly would often find herself talking a lot with both of her grandmothers. The two of them were very wise and smart women who she could trust and confide in about anything. It is important to speak up and speak out about the way you are feeling and what it is that you have endured. The wounds may have you bitter, angry and even hostile. You must practice self-compassion and release all the hurt, sickness and pain so that you can be made complete. Do not hold on to it.

Shelly was learning and trying to let go of all the hurt so that she could be free from her negative situations. All the qualities we hope to attain spirituality, such as radiance, humility, joy, a sense of the soul, and God's presence is an integral and necessary part of being healed. They emerge when you are a complete person, which means becoming whole. It is important to know that all spiritual value resides at the core of self. It is good to understand that thoughts that lead to brokenness are the devil's way of blocking what God wants you to know about who you are in Christ.

You have to take those thoughts about yourself and lock them up or dispose of them. Make your mind listen to what God has to say about you. If you do, you will find wholeness. Despite your emotional wounds, the hurt will pass, and the scars will eventually heal. As time moves on, so does the emotional strain, so don't hold on so tight to your story of pain.

People say that the past never stops happening, and they're not wrong. Every day in our lives is the fruit of what we carry on our back. No matter how hard you scrub away your consciousness of certain things, they still have an impact on who you are today and who you'll be tomorrow. That's why it's so important to heal emotional wounds from the past.

There are times when your self-love really gets put at risk because of past experiences. All the different kinds of rejection lead to suffering. It doesn't matter what causes them. The truth is that it's a kind of pain none of us are immune to and definitely don't want to get used to.

Emotional wounds with a link to independence come up in situations where someone is too controlling with you. Usually, what happens is that someone with power over you uses that power arbitrarily. But by doing that, they do a lot of damage to your personal feeling of independence. Shelly felt independent; however, with some of the situations she endured with her mom, the molester, the feelings of rejection she could relate to and notice some damage when it came to her independence. She fought against it to the best of her ability and refused to let that be taken from her.

But I will restore you to health and heal your wounds,
declares the Lord.

Jeremiah 30:17

He gives strength to the weary and increases the power of the
weak…those who hope in the Lord will renew their strength.

Isaiah 40:29,31

In all their affliction he was afflicted, and the angel of his
presence saved them: in his love and in his pity, he redeemed
them; and he bare them, and carried them all the days of old.

Isaiah 63:9

O'LORD, my strength, and my fortress, and my refuge in the
day of affliction, the Gentiles shall come unto thee from the
ends of the earth, and shall say, Surely, our fathers have
inherited lies, vanity, and [things] wherein [there is] no
profit.

Jeremiah 16:19

I remain confident of this: I will see the goodness of the
LORD in the land of the living. Wait for the LORD; be
strong and take heart and wait for the LORD.

Psalm 27:13-14

Don't be afraid, for I am with you.

Isaiah 41:10

But they that wait upon the LORD shall renew their
strength; they shall mount up with wings as eagles; they shall
run, and not be weary; and they shall walk and not faint.

Isaiah 40-31

A broken and a contrite heart, O
God, thou will not despise.

Psalm 51-17

We are troubled on every side, yet not distresses; we are
perplexed, but not in despair...knowing that he which raised
up the Lord Jesus shall raise up us also by Jesus, and shall
present us with you.

2 Corinthians 4-8, 14

"Jesus saith unto him, Wilt thou be made whole? The
impotent man answered him, Sir, I have no man to put me
into the pool. Jesus saith unto him, Rise and walk.
Immediately the man was made whole and walked."

John 5:6-9

But let him ask in faith, with no doubting, for the one who
doubts is like a wave of the sea that is driven and tossed by the
wind. For that person must not suppose that he will receive
anything from the Lord; he is a double-minded man, unstable
in all his ways.

James 1:6-8

Now may the God of peace himself sanctify you completely
and may your whole spirit and soul and body be kept
blameless at the coming of our Lord Jesus Christ.

1 Thessalonians 5:23

PRAYER FOR EMOTIONAL SUFFERING

Father, in the name of Jesus, I come to you with emotional hurt. I pray that you will comfort me in my suffering, Be near me in this time of pain, and sustain me by your grace. You know me better than I know myself. I need You to come into my heart and bind up the brokenness in me. Give me such confidence and assurance in the power of your grace. I want to put my whole trust in you for healing and deliverance; through our Savior Jesus Christ. Amen

CHAPTER THREE

PRISON OF UNFORGIVENESS

*S*helly, is not totally grasping and understanding all that she has endured. Knowing that she was quite strong and that many people could not handle or tolerate some of the matters she has indulged. Now her 40-year-old mom has been diagnosed with lung cancer and admitted to the hospital. Shelly is upset with this news, not knowing what's going to take place or happen. She is the oldest of her siblings and knows that now is the time for her to truly step it up and help in every area possible.

Everyone is now living with her loving grandmother, her mom and sisters. Decisions have to now be made regarding this horrific news, despite feeling numb and not totally agreeing with some of the final calls regarding the diagnosis. This illness was not good in any way, shape or form. Shelly's mother was convinced by the doctor that the cancer was the size of a small tangerine and that they could possibly go in and remove it without a problem.

Shelly and her grandmother wanted to hear other options as well. Her grandma did not have much peace with the doctor's answer for her child. She felt that they wanted to use her as an experiment instead of giving other medical choices. Shelly agreed with her grandmother and tried hard to convince her mother not to just settle on what the one physician said. Shelly's mother was convinced, ready to prepare and take the necessary steps in getting the operation going so that everything could go back to normal. That was her way of thinking but that was not as realistic as it may have sounded to her regarding this overall situation.

Her grandmother counseled her mom to just wait and try some natural herbs first before letting them cut and do surgery on her. Shelly agreed 100% with her grandma, but that is not what her mom wanted to do. Life was now changing for sure and the household dynamic was now contrary. All her sisters and mom were all back together again. The circumstances were not too great, but they are now living under the same roof. The good thing for Shelly was that her mom was not using the drugs.

Her mother was being prepped and treated for the soon-to-be surgery. Her mother was in and out of the hospital, going through the radiation treatments. She gathered her daughters together and let them know that she felt really bad with these treatments and that she knew she was going to live long. The treatments made her feel very ill and she had not had the surgery yet. Her mother told Shelly and her little sisters that she was not sure when she was going to pass away but it would not be long. She did not have much fight in her to just hold on. She was really tired.

She let them all know to stay close to each other, stick together and get their education. She also informed them that no one could take her place; no one would treat you like your mother and that she loved them all so much. Continuing with the treatments, she began to fade away, physically and mentally. These treatments were to see if this could help with possibly cure or at least shrink the cells. When both healthy and cancerous cells are damaged by radiation therapy, the goal of radiation therapy is to destroy as few normal, healthy cells as possible.

Normal cells can often repair much of the damage caused by radiation. However, the treatment was not good for Shelly's mother. This went on for a few weeks in which all of her long beautiful black bouncy hair fell out. Her mother was totally skin bald. This was not looking good at all. The surgery date was scheduled, and Shelly was not content, but she supported her mother's decision.

It was on an early Wednesday July morning; Shelly knew that she was to support, care and pray for her mother, along with many family members and friends. Her mother went into the surgery with a positive attitude despite all her pain and discomfort from the radiation treatments. It truly seemed that everything went downhill after the procedure for Shelly's mom. The doctor really convinced her mother that they could go in and get the small size cancer out, but once they opened her up, the cells spread to different parts of her body. Her mother went from weighing 120lbs down to 74lbs.

She was fading away and it was nothing anyone could do. The doctors did not have any answers; they sent her home to be with family and said just give the pain medicine to ease the pain. Shelly was upset and wished her mom had listened to them instead of the physician who in her eye, used her mother as an experiment. Within a few months, she was put into Hospice care and exactly five months after the surgery; she passed away. Shelly walked in on her as she took her last breath and left this earth. She was devastated and so sad. This was hurtful to her siblings, family members and friends.

Shelly's mother died just as she said. Shelly was destroyed, hurt, numb, speechless and did not know what to do. She cried, she screamed, she felt lost and just wished her mother had listened to them. More devastation and hurt that Shelly must take in and add to all the others. Despite your emotional wounds, the hurt will pass, and the scars will eventually heal. The timing for healing is not the same for everyone.

To relieve the pain reinforces the experience because you cling to the emotions instead of processing them. As time moves on, so does the emotional strain and thoughts of why so much pain. Shelly tried to keep busy and most of all, make sure her little sisters were well. She made sure they had everything they needed to the best of her ability. She decided to let her grandmother have legal custody and total care for her sisters because she was now their legal guardian.

This meant she had to go to court and make it all official. Shelly wanted to be healed and be made whole. She needed and desired her emotional wounds, the pain and scars to be cured and she soon saw the change taking place. Shelly continued to take one day at a time after the death and funeral of her mother. She was so grateful and appreciative of all the love and support from all her amazing family. Also, from her wonderful, caring friends and classmates.

This overall situation happened swiftly to Shelly and she felt as if she was on this fast pass roller coaster of life. Still internalizing and coping with the issues of the old along with current matters. Shelly felt like she was imprisoned in her mind and soul. Overall her life matters, circumstances and environment indeed took a great toll on this young lady.

Shelly was now older, going into her second year of college. Prior to college, she had planned to go away to school but much changed, and her plans were totally altered with the sickness and ill health of her mom. Shelly found herself feeling slightly overwhelmed with life in general, especially when she began to reminisce and ponder on her entire life thus far. As she thought about all she witnessed and endured, she found herself becoming upset and angry. Shelly realizes that she was hurting and she needed guidance, direction and help.

She recognizes that she has and is battling with not forgiving. This pain is real; it is at times annoying, frustrating and difficult to her. There were circumstances that could have been different only if others had listened, Shelly often thought. However, it was too late to dwell on the should haves and could haves.

If there is someone in your life who you are having a hard time forgiving? If there is someone who has committed an offense so overwhelming and devastating that you just can't let it go? There is a great danger or risk that you are holding this kind of unforgiveness in your heart. It is important to try not to hold on to it.

Unforgiveness can lead to offense, resentment, retaliation, anger, wrath, hatred, violence and in the extreme, murder. Unforgiveness not only keeps us trapped but also the person who is held captive to our bitterness. There are countless people who want to be free from this pain of not forgiving but want the person who caused the hurt to feel it as well. Shelly realized she wanted to break free from this deadly prison of unforgiveness.

One of the first things you need to understand is the concept of SEPARATION. Separation is an important kingdom principle in helping us to walk in forgiveness and love successfully. Jesus was our first and best example of separation. On the cross before His death, our Lord asked His Father to "forgive them, for they know not what they do." This is extremely powerful.

Jesus separated each person who was accusing, lying, beating, stabbing, hurting and murdering him from all of these and more. "They know not what they do." In other words, Father this is NOT who you created them to be. The enemy of their soul has control of them. Please, Father, separate them from their words and actions.

Yes, they are sinning against you; please forgive them Father. Yes, they are responsible for what they are doing; however, they are not their horrible murderous actions and words. Their actions and words do not define the essence of who YOU created them to be. Forgive them. At this point in life, Shelly has grown and matured from some of the hurt; however, growth, development, and progress are beneficial. Shelly felt at times that she was having a melt-down. This was definitely a process for her. This was not just an overnight experience, but she wanted to be free from past and current sufferings.

In her life, up to now, she had dealt with many crushing blows. There were some she saw coming and some she did not. In the midst of all of it, Shelly had been in some shattering situations. She often thought and wondered if in life there is lots of suffering; however, what is the process and help for healing? She had several counseling sessions with a therapist at the university she was attending.

Each appointment really gave her another outlook and aspect on life. She seemed to be encouraged and wanted to move forward one day at a time. She found it to be true that learning something new and doing something different every day was unquestionably helpful with her healing process. Shelly was dealing with many emotions, sentiments of happiness, sadness, bitterness and some resentment. After her mom's death, she tried getting back on track with school, work and most all, making sure her sisters were taken care of to the fullest.

It was on a Saturday evening; Shelly was at work at a men's clothing store in the mall. The mall was crowded with so many people. Shelly enjoyed looking from her store doorway out at the different people, the faces, races, ethnicity, and all ages, young and old. She saw from across the hall this handsome guy wearing a taupe outfit. She laughed and talked with a co-worker, telling her, "Oh, let me stand here because that fine guy over there is going to try to talk to me."

Her co-worker laughed out loud, saying, "Oh, really?" Shelly replied confidently, "Yes, watch and see." She stood with her back-facing the store's entrance and then walked up the guy with the taupe outfit on with this amazing fragrance of men's cologne called Fahrenheit. The aroma was strong, and the scent was pleasant to Shelly's nostrils. As he approached her, he smiled and asked for his telephone number back.

Shelly looked puzzled up toward him and he responded, "remember me from two weeks ago." My name is Bryson; she smiled and replied, "Oh, yes I do, and you look totally different." He smirked and said, "I am not sure if that is a compliment or an insult." She chuckled and then whispered, "No, it is not an insult at all." Shelly worked in this men's clothing store and she was used to the guys always flirting or trying to talk to her.

She thought back two weeks prior and recalled the guy Bryson wearing a short set and a baseball cap on that particular day. He was trying to talk to her and asked for her phone number, which she refused to give him. However, Shelly did take his number but never used it. Bryson smiled at her and asked, when can I take you out on a date? She responded and said, maybe tonight.

Shelly received his telephone again and decided she would give him a call once she got home from work that night. She gave Bryson the call he was waiting for. They planned their date for that evening. She gave him her address and was excited about going to dinner and the movie. This was something new and different for her. She was excited but nervous.

He appeared keen as she opened the front door to let him in to her home. He gave her a hug and said to her, "You are Absolutely Beautiful." Shelly blushed and said, "Thank you." They headed out on their date. Shelly was pretty quiet, just listening to him talk about life and what he desired.

Then he finally asked Shelly, tell me about you, your life, and what you desire? She smiled at him, took a deep breath and then exhaled. Well, she expressed, I am the oldest of all my siblings. We live with my grandmother. My mother died months ago, and I am trying to keep it all together.

That night was a breath of fresh air for Shelly; it was so relaxing and needed. He opened the car door for her, held her hand and most of all, he listened to her express how she truly felt about specific issues. She felt as if the tables had changed for her; she was always there for everyone, but now she had Bryson listening and he was all into her. He was giving her some spiritual advice which was profound to her. He also informed her that he was the head deacon at his church and will be ordained as a minister of the gospel soon.

This gave Shelly much comfort with him as time progressed. He called her all the time, they went out on dates, the movies, dinner, and he sent her cards and flowers on the job just because. He loved to shop and shower Shelly with beautiful gifts as well. He appeared to really be concerned about Shelly's well-being. He showed her so much respect, compassion and empathy.

Time was of the essence and she felt something good about this guy. This relationship was moving extremely fast when he informed her that when he was in prayer. The Lord revealed to him his wife's name before he even met her, and the name was Shelly. That was so hard for Shelly to believe, but when she saw it written down and dated in his bible prior to them meeting, she thought this could be true. She later met and sat down with his mom and dad who confirmed that it was accurate information from their son.

Shelly believed Bryson and began to allow her guards and walls to slowly come down. She had a new outlook and viewpoint on life, especially after accepting an invitation to attend Bryson's family church. He acted and did things different from what she was used to in a guy. He truly portrayed himself to be a gentleman and most of all, he made Shelly feel special. This man gave her a different perspective on life and some of her issues.

However, her family seems to be a bit concerned. At this point in life, Shelly wasn't totally listening to them because this guy was so kind, gentle and generous to her. He was telling her everything she needed to hear and what she wanted to perceive. He made many promises to her of what he would give and how hard he would work to make sure she had whatever it was she wanted. This made her feel alive and eager about life in general.

Dealing with the sorrow and heartache of her mother's death was not easy, but not staying isolated and quiet really helped her. Grief is a natural response to loss. It's the emotional suffering you feel when something or someone you love is taken away. Often, the pain of loss can feel overwhelming. You may experience all kinds of difficult and unexpected emotions, from shock or anger to disbelief, guilt, and profound sadness.

The pain of grief can also disrupt your physical health, making it difficult to sleep, eat, or even think straight. These are normal reactions to loss and the more significant the loss, the more intense your grief will be. There is no right or wrong way to grieve, but there are healthy ways to deal with the grieving process. Coping with the loss of someone or something you love is one of life's biggest challenges. The circumstances of death also affect and impact the child. Each family responds in its own way to death.

Shelly's mind was in another place, which was a good thing at that time. She was always smiling and could not wait to see him when they were apart. She enjoyed talking to him over the phone if they were not together. In this short amount of time, Shelly stopped and wondered if this was too good to be true. If you say that something seems too good to be true, you are suspicious of it because it seems better than you had expected. Shelly often thought of it and found herself wondering, is this too good to be true?

You may think there may be something wrong with it and you have not noticed it yet. This was something she often heard, growing up from her mother and grandmother. Here it is a little over three months and they, Shelly & Bryson, made this relationship official. This is now her boyfriend and they are now being introduced to each other's family and friends. Shelly's family felt she was moving too fast with this man.

Her lifestyle was changing drastically, and she was not spending quality time with her family and friends as before. Her family was happy for her but wanted her to slow the pace down. They repetitively told her she needed to take it easy and that she was still dealing with grief and emotions regarding her mother's death. As the relationship flourished and they got to know each other better, there were a few things she did not like about Bryson. He showed her that he was a very jealous type with a temper, which she never noticed until after they were a couple.

Different episodes occurred when they were together with his family. Once at the citywide State Fair, she was speaking with one of his cousins who had asked her if she liked the outfits of the singing group that had just performed. Bryson walked up to them as Shelly was pointing to specific members of the group and giving her opinion about the outfits. Bryson had a fit and instead of asking the question or getting an understanding, he decided to leave the state fair immediately. He announced with anger, "whoever rode here with me; we are leaving now."

They were not there long at all and everyone headed back to his car. Shelly asked him to take her home in which he ignored and drove back, speeding to his home. In a rage, he kicked his parents' back door in and as Shelly tried to use the house phone; he snatched it out of her hands and out of the wall, destroying the entire phone socket and cord. Shelly was fearful and walked to the nearest payphone, called her sister, who came to pick her up. She felt this is it, I am going to leave him alone.

She refused to talk with him that night and the next morning; he called continuously until she finally answered. He then came up to her job with a dozen pink roses and a card. He was very apologetic, asking for forgiveness and explaining how he felt and what he saw. Communication is key and he showed her then that was an issue of his. Shelly pondered back and forth with leaving him alone or just forgiving him and moving forward.

These were signs, but Shelly ignored them. That was the furthest thing from her mind because he was so charming and appealing to her. She just swept it under the rug as if it did not exist. Swept under the rug is an idiom meaning to conceal something that is embarrassing and uneasy that you don't want other people to know about. She just wanted to act as if it didn't happen and go on with life.

This was something she was used to from a child and pretty good with it when it came to internalizing matters in her life. Internalizing behaviors are negative behaviors that are focused inward. They include fearfulness, social withdrawal, somatic complaints. There are effects to the body and examples of assuming behaviors which are: being withdrawn, feeling sad, feeling lonely, being nervous or irritable, not talking, headaches, stomachaches and other physical symptoms that are not related to any physical illness. It also includes having concentration problems, feeling afraid, feeling unloved or unwanted, sleeping more or less than usual and eating more or less than usual.

This is a serious concern that should not be ignored or overlooked. Here Shelly is reminiscing on her past, her current situation and the issues at home. This was a lot for her, but she tries to stay practical and keep it moving with as much positive energy as she could. Bryson continued showing her love, affection and made her many promises. Being with him really took her into another zone of life.

She was learning about Christ and who He was, and what He was about. She accepted Him as her Lord and Savior and that's when

Shelly and Bryson began to talk about marriage. This was something Shelly never really thought about; however, discussing it with Bryson kept a smile on her face. She felt this connection was from God. By her being so young with not much experience and a student in her second year of college, she was trying to do things different from what she was used to and knew.

This relationship felt right for her as she was searching for stability and change in her life. She was in a household where her uncle, who actually moved her into her grandmother's house, was now addicted to crack cocaine. The stealing was crazy and continuous, and it was to the point of hiding and locking items up. The drug epidemic was excessive and truly out of control. Uncle James was actually pushing and aggressively leading Shelly away and out of her grandmother's household while Bryson was trying to pull her to him in marriage.

Especially with him saying the Lord told him her name as his wife. Shelly felt Bryson was telling her everything she needed to hear, and he seemed to be the perfect gentleman for her at that time. Although, her uncle was strung out on drugs and was constantly stealing from her and her grandmother. Shelly put a combination lock on her closet bedroom door for her safety, her late mother's, and some of her grandmother's valuables.

This was to protect their items from her uncle. He was so far gone on the drugs he took the hinges off the closet door because he could not get the combination unlocked. He took all the belongings out of the closet, propped the door back as if nothing was wrong, and it looked properly connected. To Shelly's surprise after coming home from a date with Bryson, she went to unlock her closet door and the entire door opened from the opposite side and leaned on her. This was it for Shelly; she could not take this anymore.

Shelly was ready to move out and at this point, she and Bryson had been dating now for six months. They had discussed marriage and he wanted to marry her immediately and she wanted to wait until the following year. She informed Bryson that if he got the job with the city police department, got them a home to live in and most of all, her wedding ring, they could get married. Bryson was thrilled and asked if they could just stay with his parents and Shelly said, "Absolutely Not!" If God told you I was your wife, I am sure you will get all we need to make this work.

Bryson asked her father for her hand in marriage shortly after. However, there was no ring, but he saved all his payroll checks to purchase her a nice ring a month and a half later. He proposed to her on Valentine's Day and then he was hired with the city police department. In Shelly's mind, she felt and believed this was God's doing. The final thing was a place for them to stay and then he was approved for a downstairs two-family flat on the west side of the city.

This was confirmation for Shelly; she was ready to just get married and go on with life, but his mother let them know they needed a wedding; he was the preacher's son and that a wedding could be put together. So, Shelly had to talk to her father, who had just lost his mother and the finances were not available at the time to cover a wedding for his number one daughter. So, everything should be put on hold to Shelly's understanding. Well, everything worked out without the finances from her father, who later paid for some of the wedding expenses. Now, Shelly and Bryson were about to get married within a month and a half.

This was happening super-fast and she was ready to move forward, especially getting away from her uncle's atmosphere who was on drugs horribly. Within a total amount of nine months including dating Shelly was about to become Bryson's wife. This was because he was able to get everything mentioned prior and most of all, because he assured her that God told him she was his wife.

The wedding had taken place, and all was nice. As time passed, Shelly often thought did I make the right decision? Was this a mistake? Was she too young for marriage? She thought he was the right one for her. This happened swiftly and Shelly really had second thoughts. She even let him know that she was not sure about the marriage and he assured her that it was the will of God. He pleaded and begged her not to leave him.

Often, Shelly thought and wondered if she had gone away to school, would she have met someone else and how life would be for her. These thoughts perpetually crossed her mind, but she would block them out. This church life was new to her, different and certainly a lifestyle that she had not totally experienced. Being new to the manner and rules of the church seems to be a bit challenging; however, Shelly handled it one day at a time. The different ladies and girls who admired her husband Bryson kept her observant, watchful and she often wondered what had taken place with them all.

He had his fan club and there were several older women that adored him. Then there were very young girls that idolized the ground he walked on. Always in the back of Shelly's head, she marveled at the actions and reactions when it came to her husband, the new minister at his parent's church.

Know that what is done in the dark will come to the light, definitely a true statement.

Shelly went through a lot of heartache, pain, emotion, mental and physical abuse. She kept a smile on her face but internally, she was so sad. She had a beautiful home, lovely car, nice furniture, designer clothes and purses, but something was not right. She tried to make it right, despite what she saw, what she heard, and what she knew. Shelly wanted to please God but did not want to stay in this toxic relationship.

She was so young and learning the ways of the church. She was embarrassed and not feeling her husband Bryson was being honest and truthful to her when it came to his past and current life in that church. It had been talked about him sleeping with many women in the church, the older mothers of the church down to the teenage girls. Just about everyone knew but did not want to say anything. Of course, he denied it and literally begged her not to leave him. Shelly felt that she could go back home to her grandma's house and deal with those issues instead of the embarrassment of her man being a womanizer of the church.

These situations were swept under the rug as if nothing happened. Shelly was angry and had no peace. She felt all alone and did not want to turn to her family about what she was going through. She thought they would throw in her face, "we told you not to marry him so soon." Shelly was feeling confused and bewildered because this charming guy told her that God told him her name and that she was his wife. A few members of her family even said to her before marrying him, live with him to see if that is what you want.

Shelly felt that would be a mistake because the teaching she was learning was that they should get married first. So, she was fresh in the church, learning the ways and wanted to be in the will of God. However, at this point in her life, she really wanted out of the marriage immediately. She began to feel as if she was in a prison.

She felt smothered, controlled, and at some points, she wondered if he was jealous of her. Prison is a place of confinement of persons in lawful detention, especially persons convicted of crimes or forcible restraint. Shelly knew that she hadn't done anything wrong; all she tried to do is love this man and be a good wife. This whole new lifestyle was so new to her. There were times she felt that she was in jail or in a house of reform. She realized that with this man she married, it was his way or no way.

Often thinking was this marriage of God, and had a misconception decision been made for her to just move out of her grandmother's house. She did not envision this at the moment and in time. Shelly now realized that she did not have to get married to move out. She would frequently find herself thinking she could have worked and got her own place to live instead of rushing into this marriage.

Shelly realized that Bryson was there and knew part of her story in the midst of her uncle constantly stealing from their household. Was Bryson her excuse to move out? At this point in her life, she was really confused. Shelly would wake up some days not liking Bryson and wondering if she even loved him.

She found herself feeling angry and manipulated. This man that claimed to love her had a really devious influence on her. It was all about what he wanted and who he was trying to prove something to in her eyesight. This caused her to feel unforgiveness in her heart even more. Shelly was really dealing with this matter and needed help. A grudge against someone that has offended you is not a good thing to hold on to. Releasing it as soon as possible was easier said than done for Shelly and lots of others.

The state of forgiveness is defined as the degree of positive thoughts, feelings, and intentions toward an offender in regard to a specific instance of interpersonal conflict. This is truly a choice one has to make. It is imperative to know that if you want to understand unforgiveness, you must first know what forgiveness is. Forgiveness is the willingness to pardon, excuse, absolve, cease to feel resentment against, make allowances for, bear with, think no more of. Allow for, bury the hatchet, remit the penalty of, acquit, clear exonerate, overlook, discharge, set free, release, wipe the slate clean, let bygones be bygones.

Unforgiveness is when you are unwilling or unable to forgive someone for hurting, betraying, breaking your trust or causing you intense emotional pain. Know that forgiving is highly recommended. The spiritual definition of Unforgiveness defines it as poison and goes on to say that Unforgiveness is disobedience. Unforgiveness is self-destructive; it is harmful to you/oneself. Forgiving is highly recommended, as there are various researches that have been carried out, which shows that unforgiveness causes health issues, such as low self-esteem, lack of self-love, and cancer.

61% of cancer patients have forgiveness issues; bitterness increased the risk of depression, blood pressure and heart disease. Holding unforgiveness against someone is like drinking poison in the hope the other person gets sick. The harsh truth is that one may be causing themselves more pain by holding on to the anger; the person that you wish not to forgive has the subconscious power to control you. Forgiving is the answer and this will disconnect you from the power of control. You are encouraged to release yourself from the prison of unforgiveness.

Like Jesus, we must learn to separate each person who has hurt or offended us from their sin-filled words and actions, just as God in His love, mercy and grace, separates and forgives us for our sin-filled words, actions and thought numerous times a day. Separation say's "Yes, you HAVE done and said some horrible, hurt-filled, sinful stuff but you ARE NOT all that sin." It also says, "I choose to forgive you and let God my Father be your judge and jury because every person is responsible for their action before God."

You have a choice to forgive, which is good and not to forgive is bad.

Shelly was at a place of imprisonment, knowing that she couldn't allow this to control her life. She wanted to be free from not forgiving. The process was not easy, but she took one day at a time, having a mindset to release the hurt she experienced.

Then Peter came to Him and said, "Lord, how often shall my brother sin against me, and I forgive him? Up to seven times? Jesus said to him, I do not say to you seven times, but seventy times seven.

Matthew:21-22

For if you forgive others their trespasses, your heavenly Father will also forgive you, but if you do not forgive others their trespasses, neither will your Father forgive you your trespasses.

* Matt 6:14-15*

"Judge not, and you will not be judged; condemned; forgive, and you will be forgiven.

Luke 6:37

Be kind to one another, tenderhearted forgiving one another, as God in Christ forgave you.

Ephesian 4:32

PRAYER FOR FORGIVING OTHERS

Heavenly Father,

I praise your holy name and thank you for the gift of forgiveness. I lift you up and give you all praise and honor. I refuse to hold on to the hurt and pain. My mind is made up to release it today. Thank you for your only begotten Son who loved me enough to come to earth and experience the worst pain so that I could be forgiven. Your mercy flows to me despite my faults, flaws, and failures. Your Word says to "clothe yourselves with love, which binds us all together in perfect harmony." Help me God to demonstrate and show unconditional love every day, even to those who hurt me and let me down. I love you Lord. Amen

CHAPTER FOUR

OVERCOME SHOCK & LIFELONG WOUNDS

———————— ୬ ୧ ୧ ୮ ————————

S helly had so much going on in her head when it came to her past and her future. She had to adjust and learn that there are other ways of life besides what she was used to. She began to really think and meditate on some of the issues in her life, wondering if the right decisions were made. She thought about how she connected with friends that encouraged and motivated her even though she never told them her story.

She was now at this point in her life that she wanted to express how she felt from her past as well as her current conditions. She was tired of carrying this weight of hurt and pain. The time was now for her to dismiss all that she's been internalizing for so long. Shelly needed guidance and began to pray for wisdom, knowledge and understanding. She wanted to be healed and delivered from all her pains in Jesus name.

She knew that living in God's wisdom fills your life with great qualities. The time was now for Shelly to make her environment and atmosphere pleasant to be around. She began to fast and pray seeking to live by God's wisdom daily. This was not easy for her, but the insight of the Lord began to help her be considerate of other people, especially those closest to her who had caused some of her discomfort and heartbreak. Shelly found it to be hard at times, but wanted to have a sincere and kind heart. She was ready to walk in freedom taking one day at a time.

Trouble doesn't last always. There is definitely a light at the end of the tunnel.

This is not an easy task at all for anyone to deal with. Shelly perceived and understood that she could not do this alone. She talked with certain trustworthy family and friends. Once she began to tell and talk about her issues out loud. It was like a breath of fresh air. She had incorporated and kept so much within for so long until it was refreshing to discuss some of what she had been dealing with aloud. Her mind was made up and she would not feel suffocated and smothered any longer.

In life, there are times when you cannot face your battles alone. You have to put your pride to the side and be humble and ask for help. It could be from someone specific or just get down on your knees and cry out to Lord Almighty. The Almighty will help you; just make sure your heart is pure and sincere.

Shelly could relate to having wounds big or small. She learned many lessons and refused to let any type of pride or arrogance get in her way from being defeated. She tried to stay humble and meek in the midst of every storm she faced. Now, this does not mean she did not get angry, upset and express how she felt to a certain extent.

Shelly just refused to allow the issues faced rule in her life. She believed that the enemy was defeated in her mind and soul. She was not giving him any glory in any of her situations. She tried hard not to be haughty or assertive. She wanted to make sure she stayed humble in the midst of it all. Shelly had tolerated and bore the hurt and devastation in many different aspects. It was time to get rid of the lifelong hurts and pains for real. You can suffer or let go of what no longer serves you. Many people mask their pain by avoiding it. They rather forget the hurt which only reinforces it. You must acknowledge all your darkness, like pain and grief so that you can be free from it and not allow it to regulate your life any longer.

If you appreciate the sun and wish away the darkness, how would you see the stars at night? Your emotional wounds lead you to experience the wholeness of yourself. It is remiss to emphasize your darkness while identifying with your light since you encompass both parts. Pain is a powerful teacher that connects you with your inner wisdom. Without pain, how will you recognize the enduring self that lies beneath the rubble of suffering?

Your wounds lie fragmented deep within your psyche. If you have not reconciled them, they grow stronger until you address them. They are the imposing shadow lurking in the darkness, waiting to grab hold if you grow weary. The mind's self-protection is an admirable defense to preserve your emotional wellbeing. It stows away the pain when you're least equipped to deal with it.

Rather than persecute yourself for holding on to unpleasant memories, appreciate that your mind protects you from further getting hurt. Shelly wanted to be made whole, healed and totally restored from all she had suppressed. There are many that want to be made whole, rejuvenated and restored. One must have their mind made up to allow your emotions to be here in the moment. Most of us know that negative emotions aren't something we want to experience.

You must focus on allowing and transferring your attention away from your mind to your body. Know that it is about you being made complete and free from the scars from old. Accept yourself and your mistakes and most of all, learn from them, try not to continue to go down that same road. Doing something different and looking at the situation from another view really helps. Accept what has happened and know that it cannot be changed; however, you can be transformed.

Shelly realized everything from her past could not be changed and she was not going to worry about the things of old, especially knowing that there were greater days ahead. Sometimes you have to encourage yourself to just hold on and keep your head up. It is imperative not to be isolated and inaccessible to others and the world. That is just what the enemy wants, so go out and be with nature and communicate with others. If you have any questions and/or concerns, do not be ashamed or reluctant to ask for help.

Remember and know that no one can read your mind. It is important to speak up and speak out about the way you are feeling and what it is that you have endured. The wounds may have you bitter, angry and even hostile. You must practice self-compassion and release all the hurt, sickness and pain so that you can be made complete. All the qualities and spiritual values are the core of you. You can be healed and set free.

Having a positive mindset and energy helps you emerge to becoming a complete person and being whole. Understand that thoughts that lead to brokenness are the devil's way of blocking what God wants you to know about who you are in Christ. You have to take those thoughts about yourself and lock them up and throw away the key. Make your mind listen to what God has to say about you. If you do, you will find wholeness, self-care and certitude. Shelly often thought about all her pain and emotional wounds. She wondered if the hurt would pass and if the scars would heal.

Many people mask their pain by avoiding it. It is important to deal with it instead of acting as if nothing happened.

> *You may feel overwhelmed, rejected, abandoned, and may want to give up. You may go through different situations in life. There are some you have tolerated, and you feel that you cannot take it anymore. Bitterness will try to rise but push it down and know that being bitter is harsh, painful, resentful, and spiteful. That is exactly what the enemy wants.*

There were times when Shelly questioned God but she only wanted things to be right, especially when she counseled with church leaders. They ministered to her that leaving her husband was not the will of God, and with her being new to the church world, she wanted to be in the will of God. It is truly important to have a relationship with God and know Him for yourself. It's good to get counsel; however, you must seek and know God as well. Here Shelly is older and really wants to be in the will of God.

Having a relationship with the Lord is necessary, essential and crucial. It was revealed that her husband was not faithful to her. He had several affairs with women and some more girls in the church and she was furious. These were situations that were again swept under the rug. Just about everyone knew but no one would say anything. Shelly felt that they realized it did not matter because she was not going to do anything about it. This was a revolving cycle that was going on in their marriage.

At this point in their marriage, they had one child, a beautiful daughter Robyn. Shelly was ready again to leave and get out of this marriage; she found out some more disturbing information about her husband's past. She confronted him about it and he denied it and said it was not true as usual and that people were just jealous of him and what he had. The nice home, expensive car, beautiful baby and most of all, his gorgeous wife. Shelly listened to him and was trying to believe what he was saying, but she knew something was not right in the back of her mind.

She felt betrayed and found herself accepting this way of life. She was a very sad young lady who wanted to be happily married. She often tried to talk with Bryson about the so-called rumors, and he would never want to discuss it. This went on for a while. He always seemed to play the reverse psychology with Shelly and she often fell for it. Every time his name came up in some type of scandal, he would always get sick or cry, saying that is just the enemy coming against our marriage Shelly.

Also, she noticed his seasonal patterns in their relationship and if it was revealed or put out in the open, Shelly would always hear the denials from him. Shelly also noticed that every time Bryson was busted or a secret of his was out, she would always get a beautiful expensive gift. Some of her gifts consist of a full-length mink coat, new designer bags, even a new wedding ring. This was definitely a part of Bryson's pattern with Shelly. She felt that their marriage was a joke to him, and he felt like nothing was going to happen to him. There were no punishments or penalties for all his wrongs. This was another cycle that he was used to. The leaders and ministers of their church assured her that it was not the will of God for her to leave or divorce him. She was still learning the church life, however somewhat confused and not having much clarity on some of the do and don'ts.

She sincerely loved the Lord and knew that He was real, but she could not live the rest of her life like this if Bryson did not change for real. Shelly realizes this man that she married had some serious issues. This his life is new to her being a wife and a mother. She is really trying to work out this relationship. She found herself often feeling mad and/or sad; however, she would continue to put that smile on her face for the people and the church folks but within she was really down and distraught. She lost herself trying to please this man allowing him to have so much control over her life.

Shelly constantly noticed his changes and again, if it was revealed or put out in the open, Shelly would always hear the same excuses and denials from him. He never played his cards differently, he just cheated on her with different women and the young girls that he charmed and most of all, manipulated. Whenever these matters came up with him being caught in his mess, he would do the same thing and deny it and he would always go buy Shelly a beautiful expensive gift. Shelly was just ashamed and embarrassed in quite a few areas in her life with this so-called man of God.

She cried and tried to get out of the marriage, but to her avail, that was not the will of God from those in the ministry that counseled them. With that being said, all of the time, Bryson just did what he wanted to do, the good, the bad and the ugly. There were never any consequences paid for his wrong. Shelly did learn and know that God knows All and sees All and that in due time he will reap all that he has dished out. The church leaders and ministers assured her constantly that God would not be pleased if she left him or divorced him. Was that the answer for her because of his title and because he was their son, she wondered after years went by.

She was taught about forgiveness, especially with all she went through in life up until this point. She was still trying to adjust to the church life and she sincerely loved God in the midst of this. She knew that God was real. Shelly realizes this man she married had these issues and really did not love her the way he was supposed to.

However, she would continue to get all dressed up and put that smile on her face as if all was well. Shelly was a damaged and confused soul going to church, hearing the word, with no permanent change going in her life. She would have this smirk on her face as if all was well along with being gracious to the people of the church. She was really not happy in this life of hers. Being a mother and trying to be strong was not always easy; however, her baby girl knew that her mom was sad at times because she would see or hear her cry. Robyn had literally wiped her mommy's tears from her face on one specific day and told her mommy, don't cry; it is going to be ok.

Shelly is tired and had an epiphany realizing that she lost herself trying to please this man who had controlled and literally bought her. She now understood that she was married to a manipulator that constantly lied about almost everything.

POSSIBILITIES "THE JOURNEY OF A THOUSAND MILES BEGINS WITH ONE STEP."

People say that the past never stops happening, and they're not wrong. Every day in our lives is the fruit of what we carry on our back. No matter how hard you scrub away your consciousness of certain things, they still have an impact on who you are today and who you'll be tomorrow. That's why it's so important to heal emotional wounds from the past. Emotional wounds from the past are also pretty like physical wounds.

They heal and then scar over. They leave a mark, but they never hurt again. Except that if you don't treat them properly, they'll just keep on causing problems. They might re-open or even get worse. There are times when your self-love really gets put at risk because of past experiences.

All the different kinds of rejection lead to suffering. It doesn't matter what causes them. The truth is that it's a kind of pain none of us are immune to. At this time, Shelly realizes that it was time for new perspectives and priorities to change in her life. She had to acknowledge and accept the truth of every shock and wound in order for her to be free.

From the little girl to an adult. The withholding and internalizing issues, the abuse, the molestation, the rejection, the lies, the control and the infidelity. These are real issues that many people face that can have you stressed out. Know that not all pain is physical. Not all wounds are tangible. Walk in your FREEDOM!

"Jesus saith unto him, Wilt thou be made whole? The impotent man answered him, Sir, I have no man to put me into the pool. Jesus saith unto him, Rise and walk. Immediately the man was made whole and walked."

John 5:6-9

Peace I leave with you; my peace I give you. I do not give to you as the world gives. Do not let your hearts be troubled and do not be afraid.

John 14:24

But let him ask in faith, with no doubting, for the one who doubts is like a wave of the sea that is driven and tossed by the wind. For that person must not suppose that he will receive anything from the Lord; he is a double-minded man, unstable in all his ways.

James 1:6-8

Now may the God of peace himself sanctify you completely and may your whole spirit and soul and body be kept blameless at the coming of our Lord Jesus Christ.

1 Thessalonians 5:23

He heals the brokenhearted and binds up their wounds.

* Psalm 14:3*

For I will restore health to you, and your wounds I will heal, declares the LORD, because they have called you an outcast; "It is Zion, for whom no one cares!"

Jeremiah 30:17

But he was wounded for our transgressions; he was crushed for our iniquities; upon him was the chastisement that brought us peace, and with his stripes we are healed.

Isaiah 53:5

The effectual fervent prayers of the righteous availeth much.

James 5:16

The righteous cry, and the LORD heareth, and delivereth them out of all their troubles The LORD is nigh unto them that are of a broken heart; and saveth such as be of a contrite spirit. Many are the afflictions of the righteous: but the LORD delivereth him out of them all.

Psalm 34:17-19

PRAYER FOR EMOTIONAL HEALING AND STRENGTH

Oh Lord, You know me better than I know myself, and I need you to heal me. I feel that both my heart and my life have been shattered with much devastation. I don't know what to do or which way to turn, but to You, because you are my source. Lord flood me with your healing and wholeness and cleanse me from anything that is not like You. Have mercy on me, I pray, according to Your great goodness and abundant grace. Lord, I know that Your Word says that You will give strength to the weary and hope to the distressed. I am asking on this day for Your help and strength. Amen

CHAPTER FIVE

LET IT GO!

———— つ୧ꝺ୧ ————

$\mathcal{S}$ helly was fed up; she has had enough, a made-up mind and now ready for the change to take place in her life. She could not go on in this marriage, dealing with the same mess. Something has to be done about it. Shelly thought there were some good times in this union, but she could not go on this roller coaster with him any longer. She frequently asked herself, does the good outweigh the bad? She wanted change and the time was now.

She had been fighting for this marriage for years and in most of them, she felt alone. She had to come to the conclusion that it takes two to make a relationship work. It's definitely not a one-man show to have a successful marriage. Bryson was once again on board to fight for their union as well until his seasonal temptations hit. This was the same stuff going on always with him and he seemed to continually have a blind eye to it every time. She knew that the time was now.

For some in similar situations, the change may take longer or it may even happen quicker than others.

Shelly had been waiting for years for permanent change and was tired of all the temporary fixes. Everyone has a story; however, no matter what it is, you can overcome all, despite the adversary who comes to kill, steal and destroy. Shelly's mindset had changed, and she concluded that she was not going to be defeated. No matter what others said or did, her mind was made up and she was going to handle this situation with God and God only on her side. She was not going to talk to anyone about it anymore. Shelly was feeling good and confident about herself and she was on a mission for something new and different in her life. There are people and situations in your life that will try to tear you down, dismantle, disrupt and demolish you if they could. Those are some of the ones that smile in your face and seem to be extremely concerned about you and what is going on in your life and household.

Shelly's heart and trust had been broken by so many that said they loved her. They were family members and even supposedly close friends. She knew about the ones loving you, smiling in the face and talking behind your back. We will call them a hater. A hater is hard to understand because they are sly, slick, deceptive and most of all, a manipulator with no loyalty. Shelly dealt with a few of them over the years.

You can't immediately tell who they are, but their true colors will come out. They will try to get you to stop from moving and excelling. They really don't care for you; however, be cautious of a hater they could try to manipulate you. It is important to wake up and be careful and most of all, be aware of those in your immediate circle.

Shelly felt that she had invested resources in that relationship because she desired and wanted it to be special and above all, last forever. She thought for a moment that this was her soulmate, and nothing would ever come between the two of them.

Her mind was set to do something finally different. She realized the time was now to focus on her. She has always put others before herself. It was important for Shelly to ensue guidelines and to prioritize things needed in her life and to keep looking forward. She had truly learned from her past experiences and mistakes thus far and planned not to look back at them.

Staying focused and being happy leads to peace of mind.

The time was now for her to look forward to much better experiences. Shelly wanted help in continuing to grow stronger and deeper with her faith in Jesus Christ. It was time for her to go to another level. The actions you give your time and energy to should help you become a better person and even stronger in Christ. Shelly's mind was made up, despite the enemy continuing to bring thoughts of the past hurts, pain, destruction and devastation. Shelly needed change to take place in her life and the time was now. Her mind was set, and she knew that it could definitely be done with the Lord on her side.

She realized that it was time to conquer everything that had taken place in her life. This is related to some of her choices made.

The time was now for Shelly to have the ability to decide that being free was the choice needed for her life. This was imperative and a fundamental indicator of economic well-being and development for her. Shelly cried many tears and felt like she had cried her last tear, knowing that the Almighty was on her side and most of all, knowledgeable of Him having the last and final say over everything in her life!

> *Let go of the pain and disappointments of the past, embrace and focus on all you can do and have in your future.*

You may hear this often forgive and forget. One can forgive without forgetting, but the focus cannot be on the wrong permitted; rather, it should be on the lesson learned. Being willing to let it go may be hard, but it will help you advance and the progress will be great. Shelly realized there was no good in holding on or harboring any hurt, pain and/or disappointment. So much has happened in her past as well as current situations.

It sounds very simple; however, it truly is a process to let all that hurt go. Everyone's timing is different, but letting it all go is important. Release and lose all the grudge, resentment and bitterness because it does not help you in any way possible. A sure sign that someone has forgiven themselves or those who have offended them is the ability to go through life without being preoccupied with the offender. There is a time for you to be free, let go of all the heartache and pain. Many people are stuck in the past, the things of old. Living in the past can cause paralysis that may prevent you from walking toward your future.

It is time Shelly had to let bygones be bygones and not beat herself up over past failures and setbacks. Shelly decides to look at what was ahead for her. The time was now to face the finish line and do everything she could to be worthy of the prize. She knew and believed what she would receive and would be great once she crossed that threshold and reached the finish line. Two wrongs don't make a right. Many thoughts crossed Shelly's mind during this marriage.

It was time to get out of this abusive and damaging union. The jealousy, the control and insecurities are what she dealt with all the time. Shelly realized it was time to take notice of this relationship. She saw how some of the older women in her family and friends went through and encountered similar situations with their husbands and boyfriends. Everything was just accepted and swept under the rug as if this was just a normal way of life.

Well, Shelly could only take so much and she took enough. Now everyone is different and some are comfortable, afraid and do not know what to do in their relationships of abuse and mistreatment. It does not mean physical always; it could be mentally, emotionally and/or spiritually. Abuse is abuse, and if you continually allow it, they will continue to do it. Let that go because if you don't, it will continue.

Abuse is the improper usage or treatment of a thing, often to unfairly or improperly gain benefit. It can come in many forms, such as physical or verbal, maltreatment, injury, assault or other types of aggression. After continuously learning and finding out specific horrible things done by her spouse, she really wanted out of the relationship but did not know how to do it and she was nervous about the overall decision. The thought of revenge always came up, but how would or could I, she often pondered. This pain was severe and she really wanted Bryson to feel the same hurt that she felt.

There was one person that she frequently thought of but had not talked to in a while. However, when they did talk, she could talk to him about any and everything. His name was Terrance and she knew him from school back in the days. He was always there to lend a listening ear and someone she could always count on growing up. When they came into contact again after many years of not seeing or talking, it was an amazing reconnection.

They exchanged numbers and Shelly was the one married, not him. However, it was nothing but respect. Every time the thought of retaliation would cross her mind or even when she felt lonely, she thought of Terrance. An old friend that truly cared and understood her. He was a man of great faith, someone that always gave Shelly another aspect and view on all the situations she discussed with him. He always respected and honored Shelly. This had her feeling for him on another high level, but she knew she was married. Shelly would always cry out, "Help me Lord" when she would speak with him. She was feeling a connection with this long-time friend.

Shelly now recognizes that every day may not be a good day, but each day has purpose despite what the enemy brings to throw her off track. She needed help and wanted a change in her life. You can continue to suffer or have a mindset to let go of what no longer serves and deserves you. It was time for her to take the mask off and deal with letting the pain go forever. It is imperative to face all of your challenges that have bothered you and held you back. The time is now to deal with it instead of acting as if nothing has happened or occurred.

Life can definitely go on from your past. It is important to know that the only way you can let go of the pain is to FORGIVE whoever has wronged you. The choice is yours, no matter how bad they broke your heart and devastated you. The key is being able to look at them and say "I forgive you" with a sincere and genuine heart. This may be hard, but it is worth releasing yourself from the PRISON OF BONDAGE AND UNFORGIVENESS. Allow yourself to let it all go. Use your energy on the positive instead of the negative. You will feel so much better. That's why it's so important to heal and get delivered from emotional wounds from the past.

Shelly definitely felt like she was in prison at times because of all the control in her household. Believing you are free and stepping out of the bondage. The key is to forgive, excuse and get out of the prison of lockdown. Let it all go. Once Shelly let it go, drawing closer to God was, even more, a necessity. She had to focus on herself and stop trying to please everyone else. That was a job all by itself, trying to please others along with dealing with her issues and situations. She realized you cannot please everybody.

Presently, they have three more babies added to the family, which now totals four-Robyn, the twins Caitlyn and Jordyn and Bryson IV. Shelly's loving children that she adored with all her heart. Three beautiful girls and one handsome boy. This right here was nothing but genuine love being a mother to these four wonderful children no matter what happened in the end. Shelly often asked what real love is, "did he really love me or was it a front for the ministry and his parents?" Shelly had prayed, asked for guidance and asked for God's grace in her union.

She wanted God's will to be done totally. She gave it her all 500% and still was not respected, honored and loved properly. This was not Christ's will for her life. It is important to know that struggles are to shape you for your purpose. It is a great thing to press on with pride and purpose, without allowing the enemy to feel he has won and triumph over you. God will remove those that try to hold you back from doing His will and purpose for your life.

Shelly knew who sits on the throne and who was to take care of her and supply her every need. The devil will try in every way possible to stop you from succumbing to the Will of God and the intent and objective for your life. The sad part about all of this is that some are born and raised in the church and as new believers growing and learning, you watch their actions and lifestyle. Again, having a relationship with God and knowing Him for yourself is crucial. Shelly watched the way many of the people lived in the church. There were some so sincere and committed, and there were the hypocrites and those living the double lives. This is the reality of the church world. Your relationship with God really matters.

Confessing the Lord in the church, but doing something totally different outside the church. Because some of the things Shelly saw and heard from the so-called Christians really blew her mind. However, she did not let it stop her from loving the Lord and knowing that He is real. That is why you have to put God first in everything said and done; keep Him first in every area of your life because man will let you down. God will never disappoint you.

Release the pain, devastation, hurt, and know that many people are destroyed for the lack of knowledge. You must have a made-up mind! God (the Almighty) can restore, rebuild and reestablish ALL that has been taken from you.

"Losers live in the past. Winners learn from the past and enjoy working in the present toward the future."

- Denis Waitley

"The past should be a learning experience not an everlasting punishment. What's done is done."

"It's no use going back to yesterday, because I was a different person then."

- Lewis Carroll,
Alice in Wonderland

"You did then what you knew how to do, and when you knew better, you did better."

- Maya Angelou

"Your past history and all of your hurts are no longer here in your physical reality. Don't allow them to be here in your mind, muddying your present moments. Your life is like a play with several acts. Some of the characters who enter have short roles to play, others, much longer. But all are necessary, otherwise they wouldn't be in the play. Embrace them all, and move on to the next act."

- Wayne Dyer

"If you believe that feeling bad will change a past event, then you are residing on another planet with a different reality system."

- Wayne Dyer

"You can victimize yourself by wallowing around in your own past."

- Wayne Dyer

"The past has no power over the present moment."

- Eckhart Tolle

"Stop being a prisoner of your past. Become the architect of your future."

– Robin Sharma

Brothers and sisters, I do not consider myself yet to have taken hold of it. But one thing I do: Forgetting what is behind and straining toward what is ahead, I press on toward the goal to win the prize for which God has called me heavenward in Christ Jesus.

Philippians 3:13-14

Forget the former things; do not dwell on the past. See, I am doing a new thing! Now it springs up; do you not perceive it? I am making a way in the wilderness and streams in the wasteland.

Isaiah 43:18-19

For if you forgive other people when they sin against you, your heavenly Father will also forgive you.

Matthew 6:14-15

And we know that all things work together for good to them that love God, to them who are the called according to his purpose.

Romans 8:28

Let your eyes look straight ahead; fix your gaze directly before you. Give careful thought to the paths for your feet and be steadfast in all your ways. Do not turn to the right or the left; keep your foot from evil.

Proverbs 4:25-27

Let all bitterness and wrath and anger and clamor and slander be put away from you, along with all malice. Be kind to one another, tenderhearted, forgiving one another, as God in Christ forgave you.

Ephesians 4:31-32

Make me as Ephraim and Manasseh.

Genesis 48:20

PRAYER FOR STRENGTH TO LET GO OF THE PAST

Heavenly Father,

You are my everything and without You, I am not sure where I will be. At times God, I know the things in life will only get better. My heart has been heavy, but it is yours and yours alone. I appreciate ALL those who have entered my life, and love all those who left in such short periods of time. Life lessons have taught me so much in trusting and leaning on You. To you, I bow down and ask that you give me strength to carry on. Without you, Oh God, I am no one. Come into my heart Lord, and lead me to victory and happiness. I follow you and only you. I am not alone with you by my side. I appreciate all I have endured because it has made me a better person. In Jesus' name, Amen.

CHAPTER SIX

HEALED FROM THE PAST

*W*ondering how you could say you love me and continue to do these awful things to me. In order for Shelly to be healed, she realizes that she has to confront, admit and deal with the hurts endured. She knew that she wanted to experience a life of peace, happiness, joy and fulfillment. Therefore, she had to learn how to heal aspects of her past and try not to be resistant to it. With everything that she had gone through, she was ready to let it all go, release it and give it to God. This was definitely easier said than done, but her mind was made up to be healed and set free from all the hurts and pains.

She refused to continue to feel weak and vulnerable; she wanted no more difficulty handling all her pains. Her mind was ready for total forgiveness and change. Shelly chose to release it and let it go, although being a human, your emotions will try to come to throw you off guard and focus. She realized coming to terms with forgiving the past truly is a meticulous process. Shelly had decided that she had owned her pain and suffering long enough.

The victim mentally was no more for her; it was now time for her journey for freedom and happiness to take place in her life. Shelly's mind was made up to release the burdens and not hang on to them any longer. Your mind must be made up to let it go and mean what you say and say what you mean. How is it helping you to hold on to all the negative issues, stop and think about how much peace you will have after releasing it? Shelly was ready to live an authentic, unburdened, and tell all life.

Enough was enough. From withholding all the traumatic and disturbing situations with her mom, she chose to let it out so that she could be free. The hurtful words said to her, the molestation, the rejection, all of what she experienced and encountered as a child. She was releasing all and certainly determined not to ever pick it up. Now, as an adult, her mind was made up to release all the childhood afflictions because holding on to it was no help and the past affairs could not be changed. Hurts and pains are definitely a part of life and nothing could be done about the things of old.

Your reaction is key to handling the hurts and pains dealt with. Shelly's mind as a married woman was so set for change and especially as a Christian, she wanted to do things decently and in order. Married to a minister who confessed God as his Lord and Savior. He was this man with charm, appeal, charisma who looked pretty good and always smelled good. On the other hand, a narcissist, manipulator, self-center, and liar as well. This is a portion of what Shelly was dealing with.

He took her through so many heartbreaking moments. Shelly often thought this man does not love me the way he says he does. The infidelity with so many different women, including those in the church, young teenage girls and even some of her family members. This was sad but true. These were with women that knew he was married.

Instead of them confronting him with his flirting actions or letting him know, that's not right. The relationships happened discreetly. Shelly always felt it or even dreamed about it when he was cheating. This was so horrible for her to go through, but she managed to hold her head up, although she was broken.

What is done in the dark will come to the light.

The secrets will be uncovered and the truth will come forth, and God's thought about every behavior and action will be vindicated.

Every time he was exposed along with the woman or girl during the affair. The uncovering, shame, and embarrassment was just for a moment. Shelly was at a point where she did not care anymore. Shelly realized that the other women and girls were looking from the outside in, and they would soon realize that the grass was not greener on the other side once they stepped over.

It takes two to tangle and Shelly knew her spouse was a manipulator, user, and one that wanted things to go his way or else. The sad part was that it was not just the adult women; it was young teenage girls with whom he had sexual acts. There were legal actions taking into effect, with much forgiving, prayer and counseling. It was only a temporary fix.

Shelly prayed and hoped for permanent change. After going through so much with him, her focus and mind were unquestionably ready to end the union. It was not an easy process especially having children and trying to stay strong and protect her babies. With much prayer and fasting a decision had to be made. Shelly loved and adored the Lord and asked for guidance and direction.

She stayed very quietly before God and made moves, decisions and felt it was the best ever. There are many that want that person to feel the pain that you have endured; ask yourself what Jesus would do? Shelly felt that way but decided she was not going to waste her precious energy and time on that. She would use it on something more priceless that would help with the new beginnings in her new life. It is truly so much easier to release it because if you don't it really brings so much stress, tension, heartache, and pain.

It affects you in so many aspects mentally, emotionally, and physically. That person that hurt you moves on with their life while you are in this distress. The enemy wants you to be bound, lifeless and stagnated. The devil is a liar with no power in Shelly's eyes. Just know and believe that there is something greater for you to do here on this earth, and the enemy wants to stop you in every way possible.

You are in a time of recovering all that has been taken by the enemy. It is time for you to be alert and be willing to follow the leading of the Almighty God. The Lord will restore all that is necessary for your spiritual well-being. However, there are still things that are better left alone, and the Lord will give you the proper discernment to know the difference. You must put ALL your faith and trust in God, for he is in total control.

Shelly had to now focus on how she would release and deal with the pain. First, she knew she had to create a genuine, positive attitude and try to refrain from those negative thoughts. Second, she made her mind up to create physical distance to the best of her ability because it helps with the process of not being reminded of the situations and circumstances. Third, being gentle and kind to yourself is important; try not to criticize or blame yourself for all that has transpired in your life. Hurt is inevitable and the pain may not be avoided; however, treating yourself kindly and lovingly when you are faced with the situation.

It is important to know that the person who hurt you may not apologize; however, do not let it stop or slow down your healing process by letting it go. Surround yourself with people who love you and will encourage you in the process because you cannot do it alone. Limit isolation and be around those that would remind you of the good in your life. Shelly had a plan and was ready to abide by it. Let the healing begin.

Many people try to suppress their pain by avoiding it. Pain is a powerful teacher that connects you with your inner wisdom. Without pain, how will you recognize the enduring self that lies beneath the rubble of suffering? Your wounds lie fragmented deep within your psyche. You have to acknowledge and admit that you have been wounded and are hurting. This is part of the healing process. If you have not reconciled the hurts, they grow stronger until you address them.

They are the imposing shadows of your pain that are lurking in the dark, waiting to grab you so that you can stay and continue to grow weary? The mind's self-protection is an admirable defense to preserve your emotional wellbeing. It stows away the pain when you're least equipped to deal with it. So, rather than persecute yourself for holding on to unpleasant memories, appreciate that your mind protects you from further getting hurt. At this point and time, Shelly has accepted and evaluated that she has definitely been through difficult situations in life.

She acknowledged all of the experiences and the life-changing moments that impacted her, from a child to an adult. Shelly thought of her life, mind, body, relationships and how the world has changed thus far for her. She only talked to specific people about her issues and that truly supported her. From certain family members, friends and a therapist. Shelly was not alone and had those who supported her that could actually relate to her pain.

It is important to seek help and not try to figure it out on your own. Seeking help is a sign of the brave and dedicated. Going through the drama and devastation affects your mind and body. Shelly had been wounded from a little girl until an adult in specific areas of her life. She knew these wounds were now there in her consciousness and also imprinted in her cells.

Our tissues and body systems are feeling our fears, doubts and grief. Traumatic experiences can truly take a toll on your nervous system when they create fight-or-flight responses. It is very important for anyone that has been through trauma to reflect honestly on the ways in which their mind, body, and spirit have coped or failed to cope. God heals the brokenhearted and binds up their wounds. Shelly believed and knew there was Good News coming her way.

No matter how the source of your heartbreak is, God can repair your wounds. Shelly meditated on God's word, the desire to be healed and free from all of her wounds.

Peace I leave with you; my peace I give you. I do not give it to you as the world gives.
John 14:27

I know your works. See, I have set before you an open door, and no one can shut it; for you have a little strength, have kept My word, and have not denied My name.
Revelation 3:8

He himself bore our sins in his body on the tree, that we might die to sin and live to righteousness. By his wounds you have been healed.
1 Peter 2:24

He heals the brokenhearted and binds up their wounds.
Psalm 147:3

But he was wounded for our transgressions; he was crushed for our iniquities; upon him was the chastisement that brought us peace, and with his stripes we are healed.
Isaiah 53:5

"Come to me, all who labor and are heavy laden, and I will give you rest."
Matthew 11:28

"The Lord your God is in your midst, a mighty one who will save; he will rejoice over you with gladness; he will quiet you by his love; he will exult over you with loud singing."

Zephaniah 3:17

"Bless the Lord, O my soul, and forget not all his benefits, who forgives all your iniquity, who heals all your diseases, who redeems your life from the pit, who crowns you with steadfast love and mercy."

Psalm 103:2-4

PRAYER FOR DEEP EMOTIONAL HEALING

Gracious Lord,

You know me better than I know myself and I need Your healing touch on my life today. I pray that You would comfort me in my suffering, and I know with You, all things are possible and nothing is too hard. You know all about the emotional pain that I have been through, and oh Lord, I need You to come into my heart and bind up the brokenness and heal my emotions. Give me such confidence in the power of your grace and mercy; that even when I am afraid, I may put my whole trust in You. I love you, Lord. Amen

CHAPTER SEVEN

A MADE-UP MIND
⁓ ೨ ૯ ೨ ૯ ⁓

$\mathcal{S}$ helly considered the pros and cons and after much consideration, it was time to make a final decision. The mind is so powerful and at this point, Shelly's mind was made up. She had battled over and over with taking action and standing firm on her decision. Shelly had been dealing with doubt, fear and uncertainty, and it will always cause her to second guess herself. Know that the mind is a battlefield, and indecision and uncertainty are results of losing the battle.

Shelly learned that the mind needs discipline and her relationship grew even more in the Lord. He will definitely guide you in every area of decision-making. After much prayer, reading and meditating on God's word, she came to the conclusion that she was ready to step out for change. Turning back to the things of old was not an option for Shelly. She had conquered and overcome much.

Shelly felt that no more would be tolerated. Permanent change was taking place in her life and she refused to dwell on the old especially realizing it cannot be made different. Coming out of this drought was imperative for Shelly. Her vision, her forgiveness for change, had been manifested. How could I ever forgive, asked Shelly? Her mind was made up and she was ready to be whole, not knowing how everything would work out.

Trusting God was all that mattered for her. Shelly was coming out of a period in her life that had her bound and chain in the mind, body and soul. She found herself smiling and putting on a front to others portraying to them that she had it all together. That was the outer appearance for Shelly in which man looks at that, but God looks at and knows the heart. Once one has had enough drama in their life, enough is enough and change will take place.

This could definitely be overwhelming and intense, knowing that it is time for alterations and adjustments to take place in her life. Shelly had been doing too much talking to others and telling them what she desired and had planned but never backed it up. In much prayer and consecration, it was revealed to her to stop doing so much talking about her issues and problems. It was time for actions to take place in her life. The talk was cheap and now the actions were going to be for real and deep.

It was time for her to tell the enemy you have NO victory even when she did not know how the coming out of this dry place of life would be. Just know it only takes one step at a time, if it is baby steps or big ones.

You are coming out with great faith, belief, and trust. God will give you a vision of how it all should be manifested. God will help you and give you direction on how to release all the hurt so that you can be totally free and be made whole. Having a made-up mind is a dynamic start for change. Revelation for Shelly was to talk to the Lord and seek him for counsel. There is so much power in prayer.

Shelly choices at this point and time in her life were geared toward something fresh and new. This was on her and only her; no one had any input on this decision for Shelly. This was for her good or even if it was any bad, she had to let it go and shake it off. She was fed up with the whole issue.

Many are walking around with indignation, spite, and unforgiveness, not realizing that you are held captive in a prison cell. It could be in your mind, body and soul. A prison is a building people are legally held as a punishment for a crime committed or while awaiting trial. A prisoner is a person legally held in prison as a punishment for crimes or while awaiting trial. Shelly knew that no one was perfect, but she should not be treated and feel the way she was. She prayed about it all and knew that she was in the will of the Lord for change.

There are prayers going forth for a spring, an outpouring or outflow for your life, but God is working out everything piece by piece in His timing. The Lord's timing is different from ours. Shelly's vision, her forgiveness for change, was being manifested. She is happy and free. She felt like the burden had been lifted and the chains had been BROKEN off of her.

Stepping out of the old into something new was so uplifting and encouraging. She felt alive again; she felt like she was found as if she had been lost for many years. Her family could see and notice the glow on her face and in her life again. It was really important for her to forgive all those that hurt and disappointed her genuinely from years prior—then making the divorce official really helped her walk in total freedom.

Shelly's mind was set, and all the shame and hurt that she endured down through the years had her bound no more. The time was now for Shelly to change her focus and get ready for transformation in her life. She was ready, not really knowing the outcome of the entire process. The ball was rolling in her life and there was a turnaround going on for her. There are many that find it hard to move on and let go of the past. Also, there are some that find it difficult to let go of experiences that caused them great pain and suffering.

Many get stuck in the past because of a need for certainty. Certainty is the quality of being reliably true. It is the quality or state of being certain, especially on the basis of evidence. Everyone is different and deal with situations discreetly. Moving on from your past and forward in your life is beneficial to your mind, body and soul.

Staying stuck in the past could be harmful and possibly destructive to you and for you. It is very important to turn your letting go of your past into a MUST. Shelly took the following steps, which really helped her with an entire outlook and mindset on the handling. It is important to recognize what it is or who it is that is holding you back. Find and identify yourself and know that you need change and need to be away from anything and anybody that wants to keep you bound and obligated to what they want and desire.

She also had to recognize her emotions, the positive and the negative, along with focusing on how she was impacted on a daily basis. Not always noticing or realizing how it could affect others around her. Shelly wanted to evaluate the entire situation for all of the circumstances she encountered. She had to condition her mind, not always knowing what the outcome would be. That is why she tried hard to stay empowered, thinking on positivity and trying to be knowledgeable of new things in life.

In spite of the wrong that she faced and dealt with, Shelly was inspired to surround herself with positive people and work on personal growth and change for herself. She had her mind made up and she was moving forward, reaching and striving for the better in every area of her life. She asked God to search her and change her, make her whole and create in her clean heart. She refuses to hold on to any grudges or unforgiveness. Holding on to it is like being confined to a prison cell.

The Key is to forgive and get it out in the open. Do not internalize or hold it in because it causes a root of bitterness to grow within you. You do not want to deal with that poison; remember this is a choice that you have to make. No matter what it is, LET IT GO!

"But one thing I do: Forgetting what is behind and straining toward what is ahead."

Philippians 3:13

*"For I know the plans I have for you," declares the Lord,
"plans to prosper you and not to harm you, plans to give you
hope and a future."*

Jeremiah 29:11

Set your minds on things above, not on earthly things.

Colossian 3-2

*The Lord our God said to us at Horeb, "You have stayed long
enough at this mountain.*

Deuteronomy 1:6

*Do not be anxious about anything, but in every situation, by
prayer and petition, with thanksgiving, present your requests
to God. And the peace of God, which transcends all
understanding, will guard your hearts and your minds in
Christ Jesus.*

Philippians 4:6-7

*Above all else, guard your heart, for everything you do flows
from it.*

Proverbs 4:23

If a house is divided against itself, that house cannot stand.

Mark 3:25

*But the fruit of the Spirit is love, joy, peace, forbearance,
kindness, goodness, faithfulness, gentleness and self-control.*

Galatians 5:22-23

PRAYER TO MOVE FORWARD

Father God, in the name of Jesus, I love and praise your name. No mountain is too strong to keep me from moving forward, no matter what the enemy or life throws at me. I will emerge victoriously in the end. Help me move beyond the hurdles that I have faced and give me the strength and wisdom to look to You. I decree and declare that I will overcome every challenge sent my way. Amen.

CHAPTER EIGHT

VICTORY NOW!

────────────── ༄ ༄ ༄ ──────────────

$\mathcal{S}$ helly had been on lockdown for too long. She felt as if she'd been freed from prison. Shelly had fought for her relationship, believing God to turn some things around. Shelly has weathered the storm and dealt with many obstacles. She had been able to deal with many difficult situations without being totally harmed or damaged.

Despite what the adversary had planned in regards to devouring and trying to defeat her in every way possible, she has realized that she did not give up and throw in the towel. In life, she has been able to conquer and defeat the enemy that has tried to attack in many ways, shapes and forms. No matter how hard situations and circumstances seem to become, know that you have the VICTORY over it all. One can succeed and triumph over the enemy and his defeated plans for your life.

Know that there is Victory in the struggle against difficulties and all obstacles. Shelly had to realize and evaluate her life's troubles and know that she has won over all the traps from her opponent. She knew that she had overcome much and had defeated the enemy in many of her lives through battles. She had to perceive and grasp that she was successful and a winner in the midst of all her struggles. Looking back at everything she endured from rejection, heartache, pain, devastation, sexual abuse, emotional and mental mistreatment, cheated on, and so on.

She could say honestly in the center of it all she has the Victory. One must know that there is a victory in battle and trouble doesn't last always. In many cases and conditions, it does not happen overnight, but that is no reason to give up and throw in the towel. That is when is it time to put your war clothes on, your boxing gloves and begin to seek the Lord. Ask Him for guidance, direction and instructions on how to handle your situation.

God will guide you and lead you on what to do and not do. The key is being obedient and not allowing pride, your ego, strife to get in your way to stunt or restrict you from your victory. God restored, renewed, rebuilt and established Shelly. She regained her life back. She had conformed to what the traditions were and what others thought would be the best for her. NO MORE of that for her; it was All about what GOD wanted for her.

It registered to Shelly that God's will and way for her life were more important than anything else. Know that when we are weak, God gives us the strength to hold on. Shelly knew that it was not over for her, although there were times she was down, but she kept on holding on, knowing that God will give her strength when it seemed too hard for her to bear. Shelly's help toward her victory consists of much prayer, meditation and listening to the soothing sounds of nature, especially with the water. For Shelly, the water sounds possessed a calming quality that helped her relax freely. It allowed her to get into a meditative state and she obtained an overwhelming sense of tranquility.

She found herself to be relaxed and less stressed despite what issues were going on in her life. The sounds of water and nature allows your brain to wander freely and it is credited for releasing a flow of creativity as well as relaxing the brain waves. This is also known to produce some of the best problem-solving one's mind can generate. This helped Shelly tremendously. It has never been proven why water sounds calms many, but in Shelly's case this brought her so much comfort, peace and relaxation during the difficult times.

Shelly is feeling good, delivered and set free! She's now walking in her purpose that goes beyond her thoughts. She realizes despite all she has gone through, she did not quit, although it was very hard for her. She held on in the midst of it all and did not knuckle under or quit. Remind yourself daily that you are a winner and you can triumph and conquer over any and everything you put your mind to.

It was all God the Almighty that kept her in her right mind from day to day. The Lord protected her and most all provided despite the wrong that she faced. The enemy tried to come up against Shelly's health in the middle of the transition, but with God on her side, the enemy had NO VICTORY. He was defeated and Shelly was healed by the stripes of Jesus. She went through a few surgical procedures and came out on top of them all. She cast out all spirits of infirmity that would try to attack her body in the name of Jesus.

She asked God to search her heart and said, "Give me a sound heart, which is the life of my flesh. Remove from my heart any evil or sinful attitude." She asked the Lord to heal and deliver her from all her hurts and pains from the past and current in Jesus' name. At this point in life, Shelly's mind was set on things above, and she wanted to grow deeper in Christ, knowing that it requires focusing her thoughts on Him. Knowing that the better you know Christ, the more you understand your life, and being humble is important. Shelly asked God to allow her to have a quality to develop wisdom and understanding in her life and every area.

The enemy will try to hold you back from your goals, and purpose but do not let him stop you no matter how old you are, or how long it has been. It is never too late. For Shelly, it was all or nothing; she knew the Lord to be real for herself. That is KEY all by itself; you must have a relationship with God and know him for yourself. Not half-stepping or half-hearted goal setting.

It is important to give God your whole heart if growing in your faith is important to you. Shelly learned that you can put on a show for people but the bottom line is that you cannot fool God. He looks deep into your heart and knows whether your efforts to know him are shallow or do they run deep. Shelly tried hard to hold on firmly to her faith under the stress of work, marriage problems, lack of finances, health issues, rebellious children and even broken friendships. Remember, it is really easy to hold on to your faith when everything is going well.

Now the rubber meets the road when the problems occur. Shelly definitely realized that true faith is constant and does not just come in and out depending on the situation. She was so excited about proclaiming the goal and getting achievements that were put on hold while she was married. Not really ever having a clear reason of why they were put on hold from the ex. She tried and was taught to keep peace in her home so that is what she tried to convey wholeheartedly.

However, it was a new day for Shelly and it was time for her to set her priorities in her life in order. And realize the approval of people around her could not determine her choices anymore. She had always tried to please people in the past, but now knowing and discerning that the only one who has the right to judge you is God, she is walking in her VICTORY. That is when you defeat the enemy or opponent in your life.

The state of having triumphed was a wonderful feeling for Shelly. A successful outcome of a struggle is what Shelly is freely managing at this moment in life. She has decreed and declared the Victory and is now free from the long battle of her past. You are more than a conquer and nothing is too hard for God to work for YOU!

The battle that you have struggled with is now behind you. Now you decree and declare that you can do all things through Christ that strengthens you. Remember, the battle is not yours; it is the Lords. He can do All things but fail! God will never leave you nor forsake you.

Put God first in your life. Fall in love with Him because He will always be there for you. Man will let you down and turn their back on you. Trust and believe in the Almighty. You have a right to Claim your Victory! Believe you are Victorious!

One can overcome all obstacles and hindrances that you are faced with daily. It will not be easy; it will not be fun; it will be challenging just know and believe you can get through it. Shelly is now enjoying life with no complaints. She has a very close friend who keeps a smile on her face. They reconnected through a mutual friend from years ago.

His name is Earl and he's a handsome, smart, intelligent, hard-working man and most of all, he is God-fearing. He treats Shelly like the queen she is supposed to be treated as. Shelly's children had to check him out and they 100% approve of Mr. Earl for their mom. Shelly had her guards up but is slowly letting them down. She enjoys every moment with Earl, the laughter, the conversations and most of all, she feels comfortable and content when she is in his presence. He's one that listens, gives her great advice, motivates and encourages her all the time. She feels comfortable with him and is able to express herself freely without feeling judged.

She is elated to see how the comradery is between her children and her new special friend. Her children love seeing their mom genuinely smile after seeing her deal with much heartache and pain. Shelly's confidence is on another level & she's now assertive in who she is. Her struggle was not how her story ended and she knew it was God's amazing power that kept her in her right mind. She has made up her mind to release all the old and get ready for the new and better in her LIFE! There is truly a blessing in all your lessons in life.

Shelly learned that PEACE was crucial. It is a state of mental and emotional balance. Having peace of mind is a great way to reduce the stresses of day to day life and can help you become a calmer and more relaxed person. Her mind was made up to allow her peace to lead to a better and happier existence in life. It was Shelly's time to be HAPPY and the pursuit of worthwhile desires and ambitions were going to be manifested for her moving forward.

> *Everyone attains and achieves peace and happiness differently, it is important to find out what works well for you and the task you respond to best.*

The Best is yet to come! All Shelly went through was worth it! Her confidence and reassurance rose along with her relationship with God, leading her in every area of handling this new transformation in her wonderful life.

> For the Lord your God is he that goeth with you, to fight for you against your enemies, to save you.
>
> ***Deuteronomy 20:4 ***

> This is my command - be strong and courageous. Do not be afraid or discouraged. For the Lord your God is with you wherever you go.
>
> ***John 1:9***

> "But thanks be to God! He gives us victory through our Lord Jesus Christ."
>
> ***1 Corinthians 15:57***

> Finally, be strong in the Lord and in his mighty power.
>
> ***Ephesian 6:10***

"No temptation has overtaken you except what is common to mankind. And God is faithful; he will not let you be tempted beyond what you can bear. But when you are tempted, he will also provide a way out so that you can endure it."

1 Corinthians 10:13

"If we confess our sins, he is faithful and just and will forgive us our sins and purify us from all unrighteousness."

I John 1:9

"The Lord is not slow in keeping his promise, as some understand slowness. Instead he is patient with you, not wanting anyone to perish, but everyone to come to repentance."

2 Peter 3:9

Salvation belongeth unto the Lord: thy blessing is upon thy people. Selah.

Psalm 3:8

"For everyone who has been born of God overcomes the world. And this is the victory that has overcome the world— our faith."

I John 5:4

PRAYER FOR VICTORY

Heavenly Father,

I praise you with all my heart and soul. I thank you for filling me with strength so that I may stand and walk in victory over all my struggles. Let hope continue to fill my heart so that I can rise and stand firm in your promises. Lord, you have a set standard over my life, and I will always remain victorious. I call to you, Lord, for you are worthy of all praise and honor. I choose to walk in the way of peace. Help me to maintain my trust in You and protect my heart and mind with your goodness and mercy. Lord, thank You for the victory that is mine through the resurrection of Your dear Son. I claim and walk in total victory in your Almighty glorious name. Amen.

CONCLUSION

*I*t was time for Shelly to face the truth and not deal with the pain anymore. She needed and desired not to be bound any longer. Shelly had suppressed so much down through the years until it was just as if it was a normal part of her life. Not realizing that all she had internalized from her past was actually affecting her future. From a small child seeing, hearing, feeling, and going through great traumatic situations, she acted and responded to different areas of her life.

Just because someone is smiling doesn't necessarily mean they are truly happy. It could be an outward appearance for a show, but they are so broken on the inside. They could be covering hurt, sorrow, and pain. Shelly at times, was sad on the inside and just putting on a coverup smile to play along with the game of life she was in. Shelly had grown and mature and wanted the freedom to rule totally in her life.

She finally reached the conclusion that holding on to the past hurts and pain was not an integral and fundamental part of her life; she also noticed and learned that it takes two to make a relationship work. It is definitely not a one-man show to have a successful marriage and/or relationship. She was taking one day at a time walking in her FREEDOM with the chains broken off of her life. Let go of all the hurt and pain, with God on her side, was the key and extremely important. She realized she could not do it by herself.

It is important to allow freedom, positive energy and God's healing power to be an innovative force in every area of your life. Have a made-up mind that the hurt will no longer regulate and rule in your LIFE. Forgiving is the only way to live if you want a life of Peace. Know that with God on your side, it is not over for you because HE has the last and final say!

ABOUT THE AUTHOR

Charnice S. Cole-Hogans has always been known as a strong, smart, courageous young lady. Who has always felt the need and desired to share her testimony of how God healed and set her free from much heartache and pain? She was born and raised in Detroit, Michigan and is a graduate from Wayne State University. She is the mother of four wonderful children, three handsome sons and one beautiful daughter.

While the storms of life hit her in different aspects and experiences down through the years, she knew that giving birth to this project was an absolute must. She yearned and dreamed for many years to complete this book, with great belief it would really help and break the chains off many people dealing with devastation, grief, hurt and not being able to forgive. Her only regrets are that she procrastinated for many years in the completion of this task and that she did not pursue her dream sooner. The good news is that it is Never Too Late to continue whatever it is you desire. She has turned her aspiration into reality with this publication and is thriving to set an example to many.

Charnice enjoys spending quality time with her family. She is an intercessor, teacher, and loves praise dancing. She is striving to fulfill the will of God by telling of his goodness, and most of all showing love.

Know that you can do anything you set your mind and heart to do. All things are possible, and nothing is impossible with the Almighty on your side. Allow freedom, positive energy, and God's healing power to be an innovative force in every area of your life.

www.ingramcontent.com/pod-product-compliance
Lightning Source LLC
Chambersburg PA
CBHW050411030726
47503CB00006B/2145